Xo -

anna
Bin

guarding GEORGIA

ANNA BROOKS

Guarding Georgia—© Anna Brooks
Copyright © 2023 Anna Brooks
Published by Anna Brooks

ISBN: 9798387851155

Cover design by Passion Creations by Mary Ruth
Photography: CJC Photography
Model: Bryan Jordan
Editing by Kim Nadelson
Editing by Editing4Indies
Proofreading by Kimberly Holm
Formatting by Champagne Book Design

Dirty secrets. Small town justice. Unexpected heroes...
Welcome to Warrenville.

Georgia Westbury was the one girl I could never have, but the only one I ever wanted. The rickety train track that divided our town wasn't the only difference between us. She was sweet, innocent, and rich while I was nothing but a dirty delinquent.

I just needed a chance to show her how good we'd be together, but when she laughed in my face I finally gave her what she wanted... I left her alone.

Until she needed my filthy hands to save her.

And one touch was all it took to change everything we thought we knew.

Then she disappeared.

Now ten years later, she's back and looking for redemption. She thinks all she needs to do is aim her baby blues at me and tell me she's sorry and I'll forgive her for what she did.

Well, she's right.

But her returning home comes with consequences, and this time, I'll do more than protect her body. I'll also guard her heart.

*This title was previously published in Susan Stoker's Special Forces World. It has been revised and updated as the first book in Anna Brooks' new Small Town Saviors series.

guarding
GEORGIA

PROLOGUE

Georgia

Fourteen years earlier.

"**W**HAT TOOK YOU SO LONG?" MY FRIEND Cheyenne asked as I scooted into the booth across from her at the Pickled Pig. Our freshman year started next week, and we'd just gotten our schedules in the mail today. We were excited to see if we had any classes together.

"Sorry, my mom had to finish a phone call, so we were late leaving."

She slid a piece of Ms. Lorna's famous pie in front of me, and I didn't wait to take a bite. "That's okay. Who'd you get for first period?"

I set my fork down and unfolded the paper since I'd already forgotten. "Gonzales, history."

"Me too! Second?"

It was such a relief that I got to start my day off with her. "Duvale, algebra."

"Crap, I have art."

We went down the list, and I got to the last period. "PE. Which is good because I don't want to have it earlier and be all sweaty and gross, then have to be at school all day." Cheyenne sat up, and her attention went over my shoulder, then back to me. "And if we make the cheerleading squad, we'll have practice right after so…" I scrunched my nose and wiped my mouth. "What? Is there pie on my face? Why are you looking at me like that?"

A manly arm reached over my shoulder and plucked my schedule out of my fingers. I stiffened because I knew who it was before he even said a word. *Beau Bradford.* The boy I'd crushed on my entire life but was too afraid to tell him because I knew he only saw me as a friend. "Algebra, Spanish, lunch, English, and PE. We've got a lot of classes together, Gigi." He leaned down and slapped the paper on the table, laying his palm flat on top of it. His lips were right by my ear, and I could smell whatever body spray he used just faintly, not overdone like a lot of guys our age. "Never thought I'd be excited to go to school, but since I get to see you all day, I can't wait."

I had no choice but to move farther in the booth when he sat next to me and pushed his body against mine. "Oh my God," I mouthed to Cheyenne. She dropped her head, but I saw her shoulders bouncing up and down as she tried unsuccessfully to hold back her laughter.

"Pecan. My favorite." Beau scooped up a piece of pie and ate it off my fork. The same fork that was just in my mouth. He'd always stolen food off my plate at lunch, but he'd never done *that*. "Hey!" I yanked the utensil out of his hand. "Get your own."

"Nah, I just wanted a taste."

"What are you, um, doing here?" It wasn't like I didn't know him. We were friends, much like everyone who lived in the small town of Warrenville and went to school together their whole lives. Beau and I had played together at recess in elementary school and were science partners for the last two years. We'd talked a lot and joked around, but for some reason, it felt different at this particular moment, ,and I didn't know why. "I mean, I know you're probably here to eat, but why are you sitting with us?"

Cheyenne cleared her throat. "Just you," she said as she set a five-dollar bill on the table. "My mom's here. I've gotta go."

"But I just got here," I argued, pleading for her to stay. "My mom can take you home."

She shook her head and gave Beau an odd look. "No, that's okay. Y'all stay and… talk or whatever."

"Later, Cheyenne." Beau draped his arm across the back of the booth, and I felt my eyes bug out of my head at what I'd only ever seen guys do in the movies.

She wiggled her fingers and scrambled to her feet. "Later, Beau. And bye, Georgia. Call me tonight."

I watched her walk out and picked at my pecan pie nervously. He wasn't saying anything so I had to. "What's going on? You're acting weird."

"Weird, huh?" Before I had a chance to respond, his head tilted to the side, and his hand came at me slowly.

3

I sat still while he swiped the corner of my mouth, then licked his thumb. *Which was just by my mouth.* "You had pie there."

Oh my God. How embarrassing. "Thanks."

"Well, to answer your question, I asked Cheyenne to get you here so I could talk to you."

He did? "About what?"

"I hadn't seen you all summer, and I just wanted to talk before we started school."

"What do you want to talk about?"

"Us."

"What?"

He turned to face me and splayed his fingers on top of mine on my leg. He sighed, then turned my hand over and traced little patterns on my palm and wrist that made me shiver. "I like you. You know that."

"I like you, too. We've been friends forever."

"I want to be more than friends."

My mouth fell open, and I stared at him as warmth spread up my neck, past my cheeks, and pooled at the tips of my ears. "You, um, what?"

"I want to be more than friends, and before we start school, I want to know if you do, too, because I don't want to miss my chance. Once we get to Warrenville High, all the seniors will see you and ask you out, and I want us to be together so that can't happen."

First of all, no guys were going to ask me out. Second, was he crazy? I'd had a crush on him since kindergarten. And third, "You want to be with me?"

"Yeah, like be your boyfriend. No—" His head jerked. "Not *like* your boyfriend. I want to *be* your boyfriend."

Holy crap. I'd dreamed of this forever, but I didn't know what to say. "Beau, I—" He shut me up when he pressed his lips against mine. I tried to gasp but couldn't since his mouth was fused to mine. I'd never been kissed before, but it felt... nice. And when he swept his tongue along the seam of my lips, I was frozen, but at the same time, I was really hot. The tips of his fingers traced down my back, and he pulled me closer to him while I turned in the booth and reached up to put my hands in his hair. It was thick but soft, and I gripped it tighter and tilted my head opposite his.

Then my nerves just vanished, and I got a weird, excited feeling in my stomach that buzzed and floated around my body. I didn't care that we were in the middle of the restaurant and I didn't care that people could see. All I only cared about was what I felt, which was a bit scary and totally unexpected, but oh so good. He slid his tongue against mine, and I dug my nails into his skin at how incredible he tasted. I didn't know what to expect, but it wasn't this. It wasn't *everything*.

He made this low rumble in his throat, and slid his hand down my side, and then his thumb brushed against my breast. Sensations unlike anything I'd ever felt before coursed through me, and I never wanted this kiss to end. But then a dish dropped and shattered loudly, jerking us apart from each other. Our eyes locked for a long moment, and I belatedly realized I was out of breath. In that instant, I saw something in his deep, dark eyes looking back at me that I didn't understand but desperately wanted to know more about.

"Wow," I whispered.

"Yeah." He dropped his forehead to mine. "Wow."

"Beau, I—"

"Don't." He rocked his head back and forth. "Don't say anything yet. Sit with me, finish your pie, and think about what just happened. What you felt. And when I see you in school next week, you can tell me if you want me to be your boyfriend."

I wanted that. *Desperately.* "I don't need to wait for next week to tell you that I do."

He pressed a quick kiss to the tip of my nose. "Good, I hope you still feel that way when school starts. This was all really unexpected, and I can see it on your face that you're scared, so I just want to make sure this is what you want."

"Since when did you become so good at the relationship thing?"

"I'm not, but with you, I know I want to do it right."

"Okay."

"Okay." He leaned back and brushed his knuckle across my cheek. "Finish your pie. Your mom will be here soon."

I tilted my head. "How do you know that?"

"Told you, I arranged it with Cheyenne."

"Oh." Yeah, my BFF was going to hear it from me. How could she not warn me?

"So finish eating, babe."

My face was already flushed, but when he called me babe, I knew it turned crimson. I swallowed a sip of water and another bite of pie, then he took the next bite.

We didn't say much, but every time I tried to steal a peek at him, I couldn't help but smile. And my heart nearly exploded when he grinned back at me. I went to take some money out of my purse, but he grabbed his wallet out of his back pocket and tossed a five on the table next to Cheyenne's. "You don't have to do that, Beau."

"I know. I want to."

"Well, thank you."

"You're welcome." He leaned in and kissed my cheek, then his eyes went over my shoulder. "Your mom is here."

"Darn."

His lips twitched, and he stole another kiss. "I'll see you next week."

"Okay." He got out of the booth and held his hand out, then helped me to my feet, but I didn't let him go. "And just so you know, my answer isn't going to change. I swear."

"Good." His fingers squeezed mine. "Well, I gotta get back to work. Later, Gigi." I loved my nickname more than ever. "Bye, Beau."

I practically floated out to the parking lot in a daze, and when I got into the car, I sighed and sank into my seat. "What are you smiling about?" Mom asked as she reversed out of her spot. I looked a lot like her. She was tall for a girl, just like me, and I got my blond hair from her.

"Nothing." I didn't want to tell my parents yet because I wasn't sure how they were going to react, and I wasn't going to risk them telling me I couldn't.

We made idle chitchat about what we were having for dinner as we drove out of downtown and toward the ritzy part of town with the big houses and beautifully manicured lawns. Once we got past our gate, we pulled right into our driveway. The big door lowered and as soon as I got into the kitchen, my father got up from his seat. "Hi, Dad. I got my sched—"

He charged at me and put his hand around my throat and shoved me against the wall. "*Holt!*" Mom yelled, but he ignored her and got in my face. I was shaking and terrified. He'd never done something like this before. Sure, he wasn't the nicest man, and he was known to be ruthless when it came to business, but he'd never gotten physical with me. Or had a deadly look in his eyes like he did right now.

"Were you making out with a *Bradford* in the middle of that trashy diner in front of all those people? Yes or no?"

Tears burned my eyes and nose and I couldn't speak, so I just nodded.

"Never again, you hear me. You will never talk to that boy again."

"Why?" I choked out.

He let me go, but he only got closer, pointing his finger at my face while he spit fire. "Because I said so. And if you don't keep him away from you, I will, Georgia. And trust me"—he shared a threatening look with my mom before turning that evil glare my way—"you do not want me to do that."

CHAPTER 1

Beau

Present day.

"I'LL SEE YOU NEXT WEEK." I LIFTED MY CHIN AT my buddy Grayson who was a cop in the bordering town of Lawless. We met every Friday after our shifts to catch up on things that might be relevant to our respective departments and also to shoot the shit since we'd been friends for years. "And thanks for telling me about Baker."

He waved me off. "No problem. I'm sure it's just a phase."

My baby brother had recently turned twenty-one and was enjoying every minute, maybe a little too much. "I hope so. And Gray, if you hear anything new or even get a whisper that something is going on with that motherfucker, I want to know."

"I know, Beau. You've made this point a million times, and I've told you I have your back. He's locked up right now, isn't he?"

Grayson had put away a piece of shit I'd been after for the better part of a decade, and even though it wasn't my jurisdiction, I vowed to do everything in my power to keep his ass locked up for every single second of his sentence. "Yeah, I hear you. Appreciate it, man. Later."

We pulled out of the empty lot and went opposite ways. It had been an exhausting week, and I was ready to kick back with a drink. I rolled down my window as I got closer to Warrenville and got a whiff of grain and woods. I could practically taste the whiskey waiting for me on my kitchen counter. My calf muscle flexed when I pressed my foot harder on the gas pedal and the engine roared as I picked up speed. Steering my SUV around the final stretch of the long, winding country road before I reached my neighborhood, a car with a woman leaning against it came into view. *Dammit.* I really just wanted to get home, but from the looks of it, she'd nearly driven her vehicle into the ditch. And the man in me, the *public servant* in me, couldn't ignore a damsel in distress.

Flicking the switch to engage my blue lights, I pulled over behind the vehicle and shined my spotlight toward the rear end. My boots stirred up the dirt and gravel as I stepped out. "Evenin'." I made my way closer, hand on my service weapon, and as her shadowed figure became clearer, I asked, "What seems to be the problem?"

"*Oh my God.* Beau..."

I stopped dead in my tracks, immediately regretting my decision to help and wishing I'd taken the long way home. My shoulders slumped and my hands fell to my thighs in tight fists because the woman standing before me was the last person I wanted to see. Or the only one. I wasn't sure which because I wasn't prepared. Hell, even if I knew she was back in town, nothing could have prepared me for being face-to-face with her again.

Georgia Westbury was the girl of my dreams and simultaneously the star of my nightmares. The woman who killed my soul, yet the only one who could resurrect me.

She shuffled closer, and I took the opportunity to scan her from head to toe. It struck me that she didn't look as good as the last time I saw her before she skipped town ten years ago. No... she was somehow even more beautiful. And all grown up. Her hair was still blond and wavy, but it stopped just past her shoulders instead of flowing down to her curvy ass. Her brows were darker, and the bold eyeliner she used to wear was nonexistent. I dug my heels deeper so I wouldn't take a step to discover if her eyes were still blue like the ocean.

She never believed me when I told her how pretty she was without makeup. I once caught her trying to apply mascara before I woke up, and needless to say, she needed a new tube since I threw that one in the toilet and then showed her exactly how gorgeous I thought she was. She almost always wore Chucks with jean shorts and a tank top with a flannel tied around her waist, because even in Texas, she got cold all the time. And that hadn't changed. Neither had the fact that her long, lean legs went up to her throat... a place I knew intimately because she loved it when my lips lingered at the sensitive skin there. Her thighs were thicker but toned and muscular, and it was on the tip of my tongue to demand she turn around so I could see her from behind.

But that would have given her the idea that I was still attracted to her, and I couldn't have that. I had to use every single part of my training to pretend I wasn't affected by her after all these years. So I widened my stance and crossed my arms, unconsciously protecting myself from the hurt only she could cause. "Georgia."

"You're a, uh, cop now?"

I didn't dignify that with a response. "What's wrong with your car?"

She swallowed nervously as I rejected her attempt at small talk and took a step closer, her features illuminated from my headlights as they shone on her. "I don't know. I've been driving for sixteen hours straight, and it was fine this whole time, but it just kind of sputtered. So I pulled over. There's no signal on my phone, and I—"

"Let me have a look, see if I can figure it out. You know how good my filthy hands are with cars, after all."

Her face was guarded but it fell when I reminded her of the insults she used to throw at me when she despised me. Our history was complicated, but I still remembered it like it was yesterday. "Be—"

Lifting a hand, I cut her off. "That was out of line. It won't happen again." I left her no choice, and she moved aside when I walked around her, huffing at the fact that she was driving a Mercedes. Figures. Nothing but the best for Georgia Westbury or, at least, the most expensive.

I yanked the door handle on her white coupe, noting the same nostalgic scent of strawberries that filled the interior. The keys were still in the ignition, and as soon as I twisted them, I knew what the problem was. I pulled the keys out, grabbed her pink leather purse from the front seat, then slammed the door.

She stood expectantly, wringing her fingers, of which I noted was absent a wedding ring. I dropped the keys in her bag, pressed the purse against her chest, and then motioned to my city-issued Explorer. "Come on, I'll drive you to the Texaco."

"Why? What's wrong?"

"You're out of gas."

If I wasn't so damn shocked from seeing her, I might have seen it coming. But because she had me so twisted up, I didn't notice her eyes getting wet. All I caught was her lips trembling and her covering her face as she let out a wail and began sobbing.

What in the hell...? "Georgia, it's just gas. We'll run up to the Texaco and—"

"It's not the gas!" she cried and stomped her feet, and I was surprised when the dirt staining her tennis shoes didn't seem to faze her.

As much fun as this was, I didn't have time for this shit. Whatever crisis she was going through was not my responsibility. Ten years ago? Definitely. I'd have done whatever I could to get her to stop crying. Hell, I'd have done *anything* for her, but not anymore. I just wanted to get her some fuel and get her on her way so I could go home and get so drunk I forgot all about her. "I'll, uh... just go and be right back then."

"No!" Squaring her shoulders, she wiped her face, smearing the tears and dust to cause dirty streaks on her cheeks. "I'll go with. I don't want to be here alone any longer than I already have been."

"Fine." Motioning to my vehicle again, I walked around to the passenger side, then opened the door for her because apparently old habits died hard.

"Thanks." She smiled feebly and ducked her head, the light from the interior shining on her hair, the blond streaks shimmering like tinsel.

Once she settled into the seat, I closed her door and went around to my side and climbed up. After turning the flashing lights off, I pulled onto the two-lane highway and drove north. It was about seven miles to the gas station, and I wasn't even halfway there when she started talking.

"Thank you. For this. I don't know how I ran out of gas. I guess I was just too tired and didn't notice."

"No need to thank me. It's my job."

"Oh, yeah. I guess it is." I glanced over at her to find her staring straight ahead, her plump lips pressed together and her silhouette was so achingly familiar. If I hadn't physically gone ten tears without her, I'd swear it was just yesterday that she was in the exact place she was now. She turned to me, and I diverted my attention back to the road. "How long have you been—"

"Let's not do this." I interrupted, not wanting to go there with her. "I don't want to do the small talk bullshit.

Let's not pretend you give a crap about me and that there's not a ton of bad history between us, okay? Hopefully, once I get you back to your car, I won't see you again for however long you're here. And I'm sure you hope the same."

She didn't answer, but the unease in the cab became palpable, and I was fine with that because I didn't want to hear her voice. I heard it every day, every night, for years after she left, and as much as I loved being able to remember the sweet melody, I hated the reminder. I broke the speed limit, and after the longest ten minutes of my life, I pulled up to the gas station just as the owner, Eddie, was sticking a sign on one of the four pumps.

I slowed to a stopped next to him and rolled down the window. "Everything all right?"

"Clear outta fuel, bub." He laughed, the wrinkles on his leathered face scrunching up. "That concert over in Lawless? It was a big one, and they gone done used all my fuel gettin' there. Got a rig comin' in first thing tomorrow mornin'."

"Damn."

He stuck his head closer to my window and chuckled. "Holy moly, Georgia Westbury, is that you?"

She leaned forward and offered a small wave. "Hey, Mr. Eddie."

"Why, color me surprised." He spit out some chew-colored saliva and put a hand on his hip. "You comin' back to be with your ma?"

Her tongue darted out, and she glanced at me so

quickly that if I blinked I'd have missed it. "Um, yeah. I'm moving back."

My jaw stiffened and dropped at the same time. No fucking way. She was not coming back here. Back to the town she deserted, that she was too good for, filled with people who were beneath her—me included.

"I understand that. So sorry about your dad, darlin.'" No, he's not. Nobody in this town was sorry that Holt Westbury was six feet under dirt.

"Thanks."

"Well, we'll all be glad to have you back. That's wonderful news. Isn't it wonderful news, Beau?"

I unclenched my teeth enough to answer. "If you'll excuse us, we need to be on our way." I white knuckled the steering wheel as I peeled out before any more words could be exchanged, squealing my tires as I spun back onto the road.

"Um, where are we going?" she asked as I flipped on my blinker and turned the corner that led to the nicer side of town where her mother still lived in their big, fancy mansion. "Beau, where are you taking me?"

"You can figure out how to get gas tomorrow. Right now, I'm taking you to your parents' house."

Her face fell, and I immediately felt like the world's biggest asshole. "I'm sorry, Georgia. I should have led with that." I released a sigh. "No matter what happened between us and no matter how things went down with your dad, I know how hard it is to lose a parent. And I'm so sorry you're having to deal with that."

17

"It's okay, but thank you."

There was nothing but silence between us for the rest of the drive. She must have been thinking about things, and I processed the news that she was returning. Here. To my home, my town. Permanently. I couldn't get my bearings around the idea of seeing her on a daily basis, so I was surprised when we pulled up to her childhood home because I didn't remember actually driving here. It didn't even register to me that I'd typed the first responder code into the keypad. I was so lost in thought that I didn't hear the groan of the hinges when the gate opened.

"Listen, I was hoping I'd see you under different circumstances, and we could... talk about stuff," she said softly. "But now you know I'm going to be back, so there's no time like the present, I guess. I hope we can put the past behind us and move on."

"Oh, I have." The lie burned my tongue.

"What?"

I shifted into park and turned to her. "I don't want to do this, Georgia, because I honestly don't have much good to say to you. And I especially don't want to do this right now, not since everything with your dad is still so fresh for you."

"I've already processed his death, so don't worry about that. And I do want to do this right now with you. I'd rather just get it over with instead of letting another day go by with it between us."

Fine. She wanted to do this, then I'd do it. "Baker was fuckin' destroyed, Georgia. He'd just lost his mom and was barely coping with that. Then you came around, and for two months, you gave my baby brother something he'd been missing and never thought he'd have back in his life. He was happy. *You* made him happy and gave him hope again, then one day you just up and leave."

"I know, and I'm so sorry."

I blew out an angry breath. "Not only did you vanish, but you didn't even say goodbye to *him*. Me? Whatever, I always knew you were too good for me, so I wasn't surprised, but to a little kid… that was fucked up." As I talked, I notice her eyes glistening, but I couldn't bring myself to feel sorry for her. Not about this. "So yeah, we can put the past behind us because it's already there. But don't expect that any of my family is just going to welcome you back with open arms and invite you into our lives like we did before."

"I understand." She sniffled. "I deserve that."

"It sucks that your dad died, and I'm sorry for that. But you're nothing but a memory at this point, and as far as I'm concerned, that's where you'll stay. Now, if you don't mind…" I leaned over and shoved her door open. "I need to get home."

She hopped down and wedged her body between the door and the seat, shifting on her feet. "I appreciate your concern about my father, and I know it's not worth much, but I really am sorry for how I left. You have no idea how sorry I am. Sorry about leaving Baker and all of your brothers, but especially you. After what we shared, how I just—"

"What *did* we share? A couple of months?" I scoffed. "You think that makes you special?" It did, actually, because it was the best two months of my life. And one time between the sheets with her was still the best I'd ever had. Even if I put that aside, we shared way more than a physical connection. She was the only one I ever wanted who I'd have been more than happy with for the rest of my life. But I wasn't that to her. No, I was just a convenient, secret distraction that she disposed of like last season's handbag.

She sniffled and pulled her shoulders back, shaking her head with a melancholy smile. "No, I guess not. I never am." She released a quavering breath. I'll stay out of your way, but should we run into each other, I'll be sure to give you a wide berth. Goodbye, Beau."

I waited until she was inside before I drove away, refusing to let myself think any more about her. It wasn't until after I got home, after I downed three fingers of Maker's Mark, took a shower, and was lying in bed that my mind wandered back to high school... and Georgia Westbury.

CHAPTER 2

Beau

Fourteen years earlier...

"I DIDN'T EXPECT YOU TO BE UP EARLY TODAY, AND I definitely didn't expect you to be this excited to go to school." My mom said with a smile as she slid another piece of French toast on my plate.

"I'm not excited," I lied. The truth was, I couldn't wait to see Georgia. It had been the longest week of my life since our kiss in the diner. "I just don't want to miss the bus."

I was the oldest so my brothers were still getting ready since their school didn't start for another forty-five minutes. She had a few minutes to spare so she sat across from me and took a sip of her coffee out of the mug my dad got her for Mother's Day years ago. It had a faded picture of all five of her boys. She loved that mug so much, it was the only one she ever used. "Who is she?"

"Who?" I asked as I shoveled my breakfast down my throat.

"The girl you're excited to see."

"There is no girl," I mumbled.

Her eyebrow went up. "Since when does my boy lie to me?"

"Ma."

"Okay. I get it. You're growing up and you don't want to tell me about your girlfriend."

"She's not my girlfriend." Yet.

"So there *is* a girl." She laughed knowingly.

Crap. "*Mother.*"

"All right, all right. I'll stop. Just make sure your grades come before any girl."

When I had Georgia, she'd be the most important thing in my life, but I couldn't admit that to my mom. I got to my feet, and she took my plate. I walked around the table and kissed her cheek. "Bye, Mom."

"Bye, Beau. Love you."

"Love you, too."

I looped my backpack over my shoulders and ran out of the house, then rushed to the end of my driveway where I waited anxiously for the bus. It was sunny already, and I felt a drip of sweat slide down the side of my face, so I moved under an oak tree for some shade. The last thing I wanted when I saw Georgia was to stink.

When the bus pulled up, I got on and sat next to my friend Maverick. He pulled his head back and scrunched his eyebrows together. "Why do you have a weird smile on your face?"

"What? I don't."

"Yeah, you do."

"Whatever." I asked him about his classes so he wouldn't keep on about me. I didn't tell him, or anyone, about Georgia yet. I wanted to be able to see the looks on people's faces when they saw us holding hands and couldn't wait to show her off.

I knew she would catch the senior guys' attention, but they'd never have her because she was going to be mine. *Finally.*

The bus squeaked to a stop, and as soon as the doors opened, I ditched Mav and walked around, trying not to seem frantic as I searched to find the prettiest girl at Warrenville High.

And there she was. Standing at her locker with her back to me. She was in her usual outfit, and I walked up behind her and slid my hand around her stomach to give her a hug. Then burrowing my face in her neck, I took a deep whiff of strawberries. "Hey."

She turned to stone in my arms, and when she didn't respond, I lifted my head and caught her eyes in the little mirror stuck to the inside of her locker. "Beau."

I spun her around and crowded her when I got bumped into from behind. "What's wrong?"

"I need you to step back."

"Why?" I asked, confused.

"I can't do this, Beau."

My head reared back, but I didn't move. "Do what?"

"Be with you."

Apparently, I did have a smile on my face because I

felt it fall as the pit in my stomach sank to my knees. I had a hard time forming a word. "W... What?"

"I just can't. I need to focus on school and—"

"Bullshit." I held her face in my hands. "Something happened between the diner and now."

"It didn't. I just thought about it, and you were right. I'm scared. I—"

I cut her off. "I'll make it all okay. You don't have to be afraid of anything. Not with me."

"It doesn't matter." She shrugged. "You told me to let you know, and I'm letting you know. I need to focus on school and cheer and I don't want you to be my boyfriend."

"Then why do you have tears in your eyes?"

She bit her lip and looked away from me. "Please, just let me go."

"No."

"Beau, please. I just can't."

"Can't or don't want to?"

A single tear fell when she whispered, "Can't."

"Why not?"

"Just let it go. And let *me* go."

I narrowed my eyes at her. "What the hell is going on, Gigi? You're being really weird, and you swore your answer wouldn't change."

She sniffled and lifted her head, then blinked and a different girl was looking back at me. "My dad found out about us in the diner and got really mad. He said I can't see you. That I couldn't date anyone."

"Are you serious?"

"Yes."

My eyes bounced all over her face—her pursed lips, the scrunched brows, her red-rimmed eyes. "Bullshit. You're using him as an excuse."

And then she lost it. "Believe what you want, but you need to get it through your thick head that I don't want to be with you. Now, for the last time, *let me go*."

"You promised," I bit out.

"Well promises are meant to be broken, aren't they?"

"Not from me, no. If I say something I mean it." I stepped away from her, in complete disbelief but knowing deep down that this wasn't her. She wanted me, I knew it, and she was pushing me away for a reason. And, no matter what it took, I was going to find out why. I wasn't going to give up on her.

"I'm sorry, Beau, but—"

I snickered. "You're not sorry. You're *scared*, and I get that. I feel things that scare me when it comes to you, too. So fine. You're not ready now, I'll keep trying. I'm not gonna give up on you, Georgia, because we deserve a shot to see how good we could be together."

"I'm begging you, Beau. You have to stop. My dad, he—"

"*Him* again? Fine. I'll give you some space, but I'll be back, babe. I'm not going anywhere." I cupped her jaw and kissed her softly, then brushed my thumb across her lips. "I promise."

CHAPTER 3

Four years later...

THE GYM WAS PACKED, AND I WAS SITTING IN THE front row as the cheerleaders all ran out to the middle of the floor. We were at a pep rally before lunch, and I leaned back and crossed my arms, watching Georgia perform her routine.

She had the biggest smile on her face, and although it was cheesy and flashier than normal, she was still drop-dead gorgeous. The little skirt she was wearing showed off her muscular legs, and was so hot. *She* was so damn hot. And call me a fool, but even though she continued to turn me down for the past four years, no other girl could ever hold a candle to her. There was just something about Georgia when she was in a sea of people that made my heart stop. Her beauty stood out, and I couldn't look away, even if I wanted to.

The cheer finished with a roar from the crowd, and the squad went and stood at the other side of the gym, facing us. Our principal walked into the center of the gym, and I didn't hear anything he said because I was too busy staring at Georgia.

She was giggling with her friends, and when everyone started to hush, she looked up, right at me. I dropped my arms and sat up straighter, and from across the room, I could see her swallow. She gave me a little smile and I tilted my head.

This was nothing new, our entire high school career we'd been doing this. When she didn't think anyone was watching or when she wasn't close, she was an angel. But as soon as I approached her, all bets were off, and she turned into a little hellion. One who confused the shit out of me, but one I couldn't get enough of.

"Dude, you're staring again." Maverick elbowed me in my side.

"I know."

"You look like a creep."

I didn't care. If I could get this side of her, the side I knew, I'd take it. But just as soon as she gave it to me, it was gone, and I craved it like a fucking drug. I'd do anything for the smallest hit, and she knew it.

"It's been four years, and she still hasn't given in to you. You need to stop. It's embarrassing."

"Don't give a shit what anyone thinks." The only one who mattered was her. And I was so close to getting there with her I could practically taste it. She raised her chin and turned her head, and then didn't look at me for the rest of the pep rally.

At lunch, she saw me walking down the same row as

her, and she veered off to the side to avoid me, like usual. But once we got to the last class of the day, she couldn't escape me anymore because my seat was directly behind hers.

"Georgia." I barely whispered her name, but I knew she could hear me. "Gigi."

She whipped around in her chair and glared. Her bright-blue eyes seared daggers into my chest like she wished she could rip out my beating heart and stomp it into the ground. "What do you want, Beau?"

"You." I smirked. She could pretend all she wanted, but I saw the way she watched me. I don't know how many times I had caught her staring, but when I winked at her, she looked away, almost ashamed she got caught ogling me. "You looked hot in your uniform today."

"God, when are you gonna get it through your thick skull, Beau? I. Don't. Want. You. And I never will." She flipped her hair, and I inhaled the sweet, fruity smell with a mischievous grin on my face.

Normally, a guy would get pissed over the constant rejection, but to me, she was making this the best sport I'd ever participated in. When she finally gave in—and she *would*—it would be so worth all this cat and mouse shit. We were almost through with school, and once we were out of here, she'd be an adult and able to make her own decisions. And once she was out from under Holt Westbury's thumb, I knew she'd be mine.

She hadn't had a single boyfriend in all of high school, and it might have made me a jerk, but I was glad. It meant the reason she gave me that we couldn't be friends anymore must not have been a lie. So as soon as we were outta here, her dad's rules wouldn't mean shit.

No matter the reason for the animosity, I missed her beyond logic, but mainly because a part of me was dead inside unless she was around.

The bell rang, and the other students rushed out of the room, ready to go home for the day. But Georgia remained seated, organizing her books as she placed them in her backpack. I slowly rose from my seat, but then leaned down so my lips were next to her ear. The scent of her shampoo and the creamy swell of her breasts beneath her tank top made my dick twitch behind my zipper. I brushed the silky strands aside and rested a hand on her shoulder. "You can keep lying to yourself, Georgia, but I see you looking at me. I see when your face gets red and you hold your breath every time I talk to you, and it's telling me something different. It's telling me what your mouth is too afraid to say. That you secretly want it. That you want me. You're dying to find out if—"

"Mr. Bradford. The bell has rung. Please step away from Ms. Westbury and go home for the day."

Georgia inhaled sharply, and my lips brushed her skin when I said, "Sure, Mr. High."

I straightened up and walked to the door, turning and winking at her as she gripped the side of her desk. Her gorgeous blue eyes stayed on me, and for a split second, I saw remorse mixed in with the desire and irritation she always displayed around me.

Strutting out and turning down the nearly empty hall, I headed for the front of the school when, out of nowhere, I was shoved inside the boy's bathroom. If it wasn't for the feel of a soft hand and a whiff of strawberries, I'd have fought back.

"Don't you ever do that again. You hear me?"

Not turning around, I lifted my head and met Georgia's heated eyes in the mirror above the sink and crossed my arms, smiling. "What? Get you turned on in English lit?"

"No, asshole. Touch me. Don't you ever touch me with your filthy, disgusting hands ever again." She motioned at me and sneered as though I was a piece of trash. Which to her and her rich family, I probably was. That had to be why her dad didn't want her to date me. I wasn't good enough for her.

I tried to tell myself differently. I forced myself to believe I was just as good as she was, but as her hate-filled venom sank into mine, I began to feel nauseous. She was the only person in the world I actually gave a shit what they thought about me. My deep-rooted fear of not being good enough, of actually being the trash she thought I was took hold, and I laughed out of necessity.

"Be careful what you wish for, Georgia. One day, you're gonna beg these disgusting hands to touch you. You're gonna wish it was my hands holding you at night and keeping you safe. Making you come over and over. These hands…" I held them up. "I'd break every bone in them to protect you."

Genuine emotion washed over her, but she shuddered, and it was gone in the blink of an eye. "Jesus, we practically live in freaking Mayberry. I don't need you to protect me from anything. Besides, like my dad says, you're the one who's dangerous. So as long as you stay away from me, I'll be fine." She ran her fingers through her hair out of frustration and expelled a breath as if she was exhausted from this whole charade. I was too.

But maybe it wasn't a charade after all. Maybe she used her dad as an excuse but she was really the one who wanted nothing to do with me. The thought paralyzed me. "You're crazy if you think bad things don't happen here, but I guess that's one of the many bonuses of living on the other side of town tucked behind the security of a gate." I grunted as I turned around and shuffled closer to her. She backed away and eyed the exit. "Oh please, like I'd hurt you."

"Well, you're acting all weird right now and trying to scare me on purpose. You've already been arrested twice, so who knows what you'd do."

I guess she forgot she was the one who shoved me in here. I made a show of putting distance between us, because of all things, I didn't want her afraid of me. I wanted the opposite. But I couldn't do this anymore. I was done. "Your wish is my command, princess." It used to be amusing when I knew it was all fake, but seeing her actually fearful of me was crossing a line, so I'd give her what she wanted. "My hands will never touch you again, and the rest of me that repulses you so much won't bother

31

you anymore, either. You can look at me all you want, but rest assured, you'll never find my eyes on you again." Then I delivered my parting words through gritted teeth, "Congrats, you won." A moment of doubt twisted her features, but it wasn't there long enough for even *her* to notice because I was already walking out.

My beat-up, rusty truck was one of the only vehicles left in the lot, but her shiny red convertible sat a few rows down, and the irony of it was not lost on me that hunks of metal so literally defined the two of us and our differences. I ignored the Boy Scouts standing at the bottom of the steps selling candy bars and stormed across the lot. The door creaked when I opened it, and I tossed my backpack across the bench. It took a couple of turns of the key to get the engine to start, and when it did, I shifted into drive but didn't accelerate as I watched her come out of the school.

I didn't know what it was about her that I found so... *fascinating*, but whenever she was near, I couldn't stop marveling. There was an air of fragile femininity that surrounded her, and something about it called to me on a visceral level. It made me stupid.

She was just so pretty, but it was much more than that... she was perfect. At least for me. I liked everything about her from the way she swayed her hips when she walked to how she was always the last one out of class because she took her time to organize her bag before she left. How she brought an apple to lunch every day but only took one bite out of it before she threw it out. All the little things I was sure no one else noticed, except me.

Just like right then, she stopped and handed some money to the kids, and they jumped up and down excitedly as she walked away, without taking any candy. She was generous, and I'd seen it on more than one occasion. Buying lunch for someone who couldn't afford it, bringing boxes of canned food to school for the food drives, and even volunteering at the animal shelter on the weekends.

That was why it sucked so bad that she'd never give me a shot because I loved all the small stuff that made her who she was and didn't give a shit about her money or family name. I'd do absolutely whatever I needed to show her how much I cared. And right now, that meant leaving her alone and never touching her again because that was what she wanted, even though it was the last thing I needed. What I felt for her was so much more than a crush. I wasn't sure if it was love, but I couldn't imagine that four-letter word was very far behind.

She got in her car and drove away, putting on her blinker and turned right out of the parking lot to the affluent part of town. I headed left, past the railroad tracks, to the neighborhoods where all the middle- and low-class families lived. Which was also something that made me curious. She mentioned several times that her father had warned her off me because I was dangerous.

Yeah, I got in some hot water a couple of years ago for smoking pot with some friends, but I wasn't arrested. And then again the following year, I got in trouble because some bullies were picking on my brother, so I had to set them straight. I did get thrown in the back of a cop car then, but I didn't think that was enough to deem me dangerous. I guess to a high-powered investment banker in our community whose family could buy the entire town, anything but white collar was a threat to his princess.

It didn't take me long to get to my dad's shop, and when I pulled up, I noticed Baker, my youngest brother, was there. He was sick this morning, so he must have stayed home, which meant hanging out at the shop and sleeping on the couch in our dad's office so our mom could get her rest since she worked the third shift at a nursing home.

After making sure all five of her boys, plus her husband, were ready in the morning and off to where they needed to be, she got some sleep during the day until it was time for everyone to come home. We ate a home-cooked meal together, and then she went back to work. I didn't know how she did it, but somehow, she managed.

Baker ran out of the open bay and was pulling my door open before I even got the chance. "Hi, Beau."

"Hey, Buddy. How are you feeling?"

"Still sick. Can you take me home?" he whined. "I want to go to my bed, but Dad couldn't leave and—"

I rubbed the top of his head after I got my feet on the ground. "Yeah, I'll take you. Just let me talk to Dad real quick because this morning he told me he needed my help. Hop up in the truck and I'll be back in a few."

"Okay."

"Pop." I called my dad's name when I walked into the first bay of our family's shop, Bradford and Sons. When the garage was started by my grandfather almost thirty years ago, it was Bradford and Son, and then when he passed, my dad took over and made son plural. It was something I was proud to be a part of and hoped we could keep it running for generations to come.

Ninety-nine percent of the town supported us by coming here for service, and even people from over in Lawless came because we were trustworthy. We sponsored Little League and always ran the ring toss game during the town fair. And every time we were out as a family, somebody came up to my dad and talked to him, so I knew he was well liked.

Dad slid out from beneath the hood of a sedan and wiped his brow with his forearm, trailing a streak of oil across his face that settled into the lines on his forehead. "Hey, son."

"You want me to take Baker home and then come back to help you finish up?"

"No. As long as I know you're home to take care of him, I'll just work a little later tonight. He's feeling better and hasn't puked since about noon so I think he's almost out of the woods."

Instead of saying what I wanted to say—that he had another son, two actually, who were old enough to look after Baker so I could lend a hand here—I simply nodded. "Okay. Call me if you need anything."

"Will do. Thanks, Beau. And check in on your mother, too, please. She wasn't feeling well, either."

"Of course." As I walked away, I mentally counted the number of cars still left to be serviced today and shook my head, knowing Dad would be working until at least ten o'clock tonight.

Baker was practically asleep, so he startled when I asked, "Ready to go home?"

"Yeah. I'm really tired, and the couch in Dad's office isn't comfortable."

"I know, buddy. We've all been there. Buckle up so I can get you to your own bed." I buckled in my own seat belt, and by the time I made it home, he was passed out. As quietly as I could, I opened his door and then carried him to his room. Once I laid him down, I tossed a blanket over his lanky body and closed his blinds. On my way to the kitchen, I stopped at my parents' room and quietly knocked on the door.

"Come in."

I opened it a crack and stuck my head in. "Hey, Ma."

"Hi, baby. How was your day?" She pushed some of her dirty blond hair off her face and smiled; the dimples in her cheeks a trademark of hers. She always joked that her boys made her smile so much her dimples had gotten bigger over the years.

"Good. Brought Baker home. He's sleeping."

"Thank you. I wasn't feeling good today, so I really needed the sleep. Otherwise, I would have watched him."

She pressed a hand to her stomach, and I tilted my

head. I hoped she hadn't caught the same flu bug as Baker had, but I knew it was going around. "Are you feeling better?"

"Kind of. I need to get up and make you all supper before I go into work, though, so I have to be, don't I?"

I rolled my eyes and motioned for her to lie back down when she started to get up. "Go back to sleep. I can make supper."

"No, it's fine. I'll be—"

"Ma, go to sleep. If you've got what he does, you don't want to give it to all of us anyway."

She put a hand to her chest. "Such a good boy. I'm so proud of the man you're becoming."

"Thanks. Get some sleep."

"Thank you. Love you, Beau."

"Same."

After closing her door, I went straight to the kitchen and rummaged through the cupboards to find something to make for everyone. I didn't mind the responsibility being on my shoulders since I was the eldest of five boys, but it frustrated me that I was the only one who ever stepped up.

It wasn't as if they were all ten like Baker. Brody was sixteen, but he was in sports right now, so he had practice before and after school. Brock was fifteen, but he had responsibilities at the martial arts studio. As a brown belt, he had to teach classes in order to get his black belt, so he was busy with that. And at just twelve, Bear was the only one with an excuse, which was why he pretty much only came home from school, snacked on whatever food he could find, and then hung out with his friends until the streetlights came on.

It was a long night, and after everyone came home and ate, I disappeared to my room to do my homework. My mom came in and said goodbye since she was leaving for work, which I wasn't happy about because she didn't look too good.

With my nose in a book, I apparently nodded off writing an essay for English lit because I was awoken from a dream of an angel with long, wavy, blond hair, pink cheeks, and a sweet, shy smile, and brought straight into a nightmare by my father's ravaged expression. "Beau... Beau, son. I need you to get your brothers and meet me down at the hospital."

I threw my book on the ground as I jumped to my feet. "What? Why?"

"There's been an accident, son. It's your mother."

CHAPTER 4

Georgia

Three months later

T HE DJ PLAYED A SLOW SONG, AND I TRIED TO GET
off the dance floor and away from Tad, but he must
have been watching me with my friends because he
grabbed my arm and pulled me back into the crowd. "It's
the last dance. We can't go yet."

"Fine."

I laid my hands on his chest and kept as far away from
him as I could. My dad made me go to prom with Tad,
and every second I spent with him was miserable. I would
have rather stayed home and missed the night every senior
in high school had looked forward to since they walked
through the doors their first day, freshman year than come
with him. But I wasn't given a choice.

I hardly knew Tad Clancy, but for some reason, he
decided to start talking to me this year and wasn't sub-
tle about his intentions. I told him straight out that I
didn't want to be his girlfriend, but he was persistent. His

attempts were teetering on the edge of creepy, whereas Beau's were something I secretly looked forward to.

"Come here." Tad yanked me closer and I turned my head, locking eyes with Beau for the first time in months.

I was surprised to see him here since he had hardly been to school since his mom died. The dance was almost over and it was the first time I'd seen him all evening. And damn, he was hot. Hotter than all the other guys who were in suits.

The disco lights bounced all around, the colorful rays spinning and glowing in a dazzling array across the dance floor. He was just wearing a pair of worn-out jeans and a black T-shirt, but he looked like he should be a cover model in a magazine. Leaning on the wall, he had his arms crossed and his fixed stare was on me. He was the perfect height, had enough muscles that you knew he worked out but not *too much,* his hair was dark just like his intense eyes. Beau Bradford was the total package, from head to toe, and seeing him across the room, his eyes never leaving mine, made my stomach flip.

My lips parted, and I wanted to call him, wanted him to come and take me away, but he didn't move an inch. Tad spun me around, and when I twisted my head to find Beau again, he was gone.

I felt the backs of my eyes start to burn but Tad's roaming fingers snapped me back to reality. "Stop."

"Stop what?" he asked.

"Touching me."

He chuckled, and slid his hands up to my back, but

didn't take them off me and I felt nauseous. As soon as the song was over, he wrapped his fingers around my arm and kept me close as we made our way to his car.

Everyone was going to an after-party at the Donovan's house, and unfortunately that meant Tad was my ride. He tried to talk to me on the way there, but I just stared out the window and counted down the seconds until I could get away from him. I planned on having Cheyenne and her boyfriend Gage give me a ride home after the party.

I'd packed a bag, and as soon as we got inside, I changed into a pair of shorts and a T-shirt, just like most of the girls. Some put on swimsuits and went into the pool and a few kept their dresses on, but I was itchy all night and couldn't wait to get out of it.

I spotted Tad outside with a few other guys, so I went to the living room and stopped dead in my tracks when I saw Beau in the kitchen standing around the keg where a bunch of high school students were gathered round.

He didn't drink anything; he just stood there and talked, and when a few girls came up to him and tried to flirt, he simply shook his head at them. Over the years, he'd gone to a few school dances with other girls, but as far as I knew, he never had a girlfriend. But even seeing him with anyone else made me want to cry thinking about my dad getting in the way of what could have been the most precious relationship of my life. I didn't date at all. Mostly because I didn't want to unless it was with Beau, but also because I needed to keep up the image so I didn't hurt him any more than I already had. The last thing I wanted was for him to see me hanging out with a guy, especially because of why I broke my promise in the first place.

It had only been about ten minutes since he arrived, but from the way he seemed agitated to even be here, I was guessing he was going to take off soon.

I needed to clear the air between us. I hadn't had the opportunity to talk to him since I heard the news of his mother's accident, but I was afraid to move. After our last heated exchange in the school bathroom, I was afraid he'd actually do what I asked and pretend I didn't exist. "Just go do it."

I startled when Cheyenne nudged me with her elbow. "Do what?"

"Go talk to him."

"What makes you think I want to do that?" She was the only one who knew everything and had been my rock when I didn't think I could do it any longer.

Physically, Cheyenne was the opposite of me in almost every way. With thick dark hair and pretty brown eyes, she was short and a little plump. I loved sleeping over at her house because her dad was so awesome, and mine had gotten meaner by the minute. "Because you haven't been able to take your eyes off him since he got here. You've obviously got something to say to him, so go do it."

"I just want to tell him I'm sorry about his mom," I fibbed. In actuality, I wanted to tell him so much more.

"I'm sure he wouldn't mind."

She gave my arm a squeeze and moved past me when Gage whistled at her from across the room. If I wasn't so busy with my own internal battle, I'd have told her to have more respect for herself than being treated like a dog. But who was I to give anyone relationship advice?

When I turned my head back, Beau was striding toward the front door, and I knew I had to take a chance. After sucking in a breath, I followed him, and when I opened the door, I found him leaning on the railing with both hands, his head hung low. He looked... *defeated*, so unlike the confident, cocky guy I knew.

I stepped out onto the porch and closed the door behind me, thankful he was alone. He didn't move a muscle, and I wasn't sure if he was ignoring me or just so lost in thought that he didn't hear me, so I got closer. "Hey, are you okay?"

"Go away, Georgia," he answered immediately. So I guess he *was* just ignoring me.

I hated this so much. I missed him not only as what I knew would have been the best boyfriend, but as a friend as well. "Beau."

"I said go away. Don't act like you care about me now. I disgust you, remember? My family's trash, I'm dangerous, and you're too good for me. My mom dying doesn't change anything." He pinned me with an ice-cold stare that made me wish I'd worn a sweater. "So go back inside to your little rich boy and leave me the hell alone."

"But—"

He turned so fast that I gasped as I stumbled from the rage simmering just below the surface. Rage and fury that

43

were *this* close to being unleashed. I'd never seen that look on him before, and it scared the crap out of me.

His head reared back, and his features softened. "You know I'd never hurt you, but I need you to go away, Georgia."

"I... I just wanted to say I'm sorry, about your mom."

"You said it. Now leave. Please."

"Okay, Beau." I swallowed nervously, but before I turned around, I stopped and stared at him. At the loneliness he must have felt, at the unmistakable sadness, at the sheer disdain he had for me. I'd asked myself so many times over the years what would have happened if I ignored my dad and told Beau everything. That after the first time my father wrapped his fingers around my throat it had only gotten worse. He'd reminded me almost every time he saw me that I had to stay away from Beau and threatened brutal consequences if I defied him. So I couldn't risk it, not for me, but for *Beau*. I'd learned the hard way that Holt Westbury was not a nice man, and I couldn't let Beau find out just how evil he was.

"What?" he snapped. "What the hell are you looking at?"

Choking down any more words that likely would have made the situation worse, I escaped back inside. But for a split second, I wanted to plead for his forgiveness for hurting him so badly, even though I knew it'd only be for my benefit. He'd been through too much for me to be selfish and try to get him to stop hating me right now, but I didn't know if I'd ever get the chance again. Maybe someday, but I knew it wouldn't be tonight.

When I closed the door behind me and headed back to the living room where everyone was hanging out and dancing, I was suddenly dizzy with the noise level and flashing lights.

I felt suffocated by my surroundings and just wanted to go home. So I searched for Cheyenne and Gage, but couldn't find them anywhere. As I was perusing the faces in the crowd, I noticed a staircase and beelined in that direction. Making my way up the steps, I had hoped to find Cheyenne there.

However, as I reached the top, Tad emerged out of what I assumed was a bathroom since he was still zipping up his jeans.

Perfect.

"Hey, there she is." He sauntered toward me a little wobbly on his feet, and I offered the best attempt of a smile I could.

"I'm just looking for Cheyenne and Gage to take me home. I'm tired. And I don't feel well." I added the last sentence, hoping to give him a sufficient enough explanation so he didn't put up a fight.

Reaching for my hand, he tugged me toward him. "Are you okay?" His brown eyes moved over my face, and for a second, I thought he was really concerned.

"Yeah, I just want to go home so I can get some sleep."

He looked to his left. "I saw them leave like five minutes ago so I'll take you when I'm ready. There's a bed in there. Why don't you take a nap for a little while? I'll join you."

Cheyenne wouldn't have left me without saying good-bye. I shook my head, but he pulled me in the direction of the bedroom. My feet skidded as I tried to hold back, but he yanked at my arm. "Ow."

"Here." He reached the threshold of the room, and a thick, sour feeling coated my throat.

"No. I want to go," I protested and tried to get away, but he used both hands to grab my biceps, hauling me against the wall so hard my head snapped back and smashed against it. "Stop it, Tad!"

He kicked my feet apart, and I opened my mouth to scream, but he covered it with his own. In a matter of seconds, his entire body pressed into mine. He forced me immobile, and I was unable to breathe for a multitude of reasons.

"Georgia, don't act like this. You know you want it." He lifted his head away to mutter against my mouth, making me gag from the disgusting stench of stale beer and cheap tobacco. "I know you want *me*."

When I tried to argue with him, he covered my lips again and then stuck his hand up my shirt. I shook my head, but he pressed harder. His fingers slid under my bra, and he squeezed my nipple painfully. The terrible sensation made me gasp even though I couldn't drag in any air, but he just did it again. Harder. Nobody had ever touched me there, and I never expected the first time someone did it would be like this. It was all happening so fast, and

I was so surprised by his behavior that I didn't even know how to react.

I knew something was off with him, but I never, ever thought he'd do this.

"Stop," I mumbled through his nails digging into my cheeks, but he ignored me.

His fingers slid down, and he pressed the palm of his hand between my legs even though I was trying to hold them together so tight my muscles felt like a rope about to snap. "Don't be a frigid little bitch, Georgia."

He went back up under my shirt and reached around to undo the clasp of my bra. "You better get used to this 'cause I ain't goin' anywhere for a long, long time, and neither are you," he warned.

My body stiffened, and my breath froze at the implication.

"Oh no. Daddy didn't tell you yet, did he?"

"Tell me what?"

"That he's been saving you for me." He bit my jaw. Hard. "And I'm done waiting."

A fresh wave of terror washed through me and I choked down a sob as I fought with him. I kicked my feet and squirmed and tried to push him off, but he was just too strong. Every time I tried to move, my head ground against the wall. My brain was throbbing, and my arms were sore from flailing against him. "I knew it when you changed into these little shorts. This tight-ass shirt. You're teasing me again like you did all night in your slutty dress."

I sobbed even harder now, and when Tad lowered the

zipper of my shorts, I tried one more time to fight him. He laughed at my attempt and threw me on the bed so my chest molded into the mattress. Following me down, he dropped his heavy body against me, making it impossible to get in air.

As my eyes began to get heavy and dizziness crept in, I went from feeling everything to being lifeless knowing what was about to happen. Not just physically, but from the bitter truth about everything that had led up to this. It had all been part of my dad's grand plan all along. Holt forbade me from dating, from being so vapid about Beau. He was using me. I was nothing more than a business transaction, and even though I was about to be raped, everything started to make sense despite the queasiness.

"Please, Tad. Stop it." I was getting weaker, and I felt my fight fading away.

"I'm just getting started."

"I wouldn't do that if I were you." Even though Tad was crushing me, and I was beginning to see stars, breath filled my lungs when Beau's deep voice penetrated the fog.

"What are you gonna do, Beau?"

"We both know what I'm gonna do, so unless you want me to do it to you, back the fuck off and let her go." His voice was louder, closer. Angry. A different anger than had been directed toward me on the deck.

Tad sneered. "I ain't leaving her alone 'cause she's mine, so just get the fuck out. If you don't and you're stupid enough to lay a hand on me, I'll have you arrested."

He would too; his dad was a judge, so he got away with any and everything.

It was silent for what felt like eternity, and when I heard Beau murmur, "Okay." I thought he was leaving me, and defeat clogged my throat. I listened for his footsteps to fade, but then a whoosh sounded just seconds before a loud crunch and the heavy, hot weight of Tad was replaced with a bitter chill. I wheezed and scrambled to my shaky legs, and saw him knocked out on the floor with a trickle of blood leaking from his nose.

Beau stood a couple of feet away, wiping his hand with disgust. When he glanced at me, the sharp lines smoothed out a little bit, and it made me hiccup. "Beau."

He rushed over to me and pulled me into his arms, providing a refuge that made me feel safer than I ever had in four years. "It's okay." He reassured me. I felt his lips press into the top of my head and I cried for a different reason. "Shh. I've got you."

I needed to get out of here—I needed to get *Beau* out of here. I pulled back and wiped my cheeks, wincing when I grazed the swollen area that Tad caused, and Beau's eyes squinted.

"The fucker hit you?"

I nodded and his jaw clenched right before he kicked Tad between the legs. Really hard. Even though it would have appeared he was passed out, he still groaned as his body jerked from the impact. "We should call the cops." He turned, but I found strength to lunge at him, grabbing his muscular arm.

"No. We can't. Please, don't. I just want to leave. Can you give me a ride?" I sniffled, pulling my clothes back together. "Please."

He stopped so fast that I ran into him, but he steadied me with a hand to my waist. Despite the sheer terror I just experienced, his touch warmed my skin. His dark eyes moved over my face. I probably had makeup running down my cheeks and lipstick smeared across my mouth, but he was looking at me like... like I was the most beautiful girl in the world. "You want me to help you? Me? Beau Bradford. Dirtbag extraordinaire?" And even though his words contradicted his actions, he was the only one I wanted. The only one I trusted.

"Beau, please. He was my ride. And I can't call the cops, you know he'll never get in trouble but knowing my luck he'll turn it on me and I'll be the one punished. I just wanna go. Please." I begged him, and I didn't care how desperate it made me sound. "Please just get me out of here."

He glanced down at Tad and then pressed his lips together. Finding my eyes again, he sighed and then jerked his chin. "Fine."

"Thank you."

Following him, I was grateful he acted as a shield and led me out the side exit to avoid any prying glances. Not because I was with him, but because I looked like I'd been assaulted, and I didn't want anybody else knowing. When he opened my door for me, I silently thanked him with a weak upturn of my lips and buckled my seatbelt, waiting for him to get into his old, beat-up pickup truck. It smelled of oil and spice mixed with a little bit of leather... it smelled like *Beau*. He pulled away from the curb and drove, each thump of the tires on the gravel taking us farther and farther away from the worst night of my life.

If Beau hadn't shown up when he did... I shuddered, refusing to even go there. Gradually, I felt some of the tension releasing from my spine. I wasn't sure if he sensed I needed the quiet or if he just didn't want to talk, but either way I appreciated his calm demeanor.

"Shit!" I yelled when he pulled up to the gate to my subdivision. Seeing all the cars lined up reminded me of what tonight was. "I forgot about the dinner party my parents were having. I can't go inside like this!" I gestured toward my ripped shirt and throbbing face. I'd rather have not gone in there anyway because my dad was home, which was more uncommon than not. I had no clue where he was half the time, and I didn't care. I just knew my life was so much better when he wasn't around.

"Why can't you go in?"

"My dad... he, he—"

"He what?"

I swallowed and forced the words out, each letter scratching at my dry throat, but it hurt my heart even more to admit, "He'd be embarrassed in front of his friends, and he—"

"He'd be embarrassed that his daughter was nearly *raped*? That's the most fucked-up thing I've ever heard."

"You don't know the half of it, Beau. Please, just get me out of here."

He shook his head with a huff and turned in a half circle. "Where do you want me to take you?"

I thought about it for a second and realized I didn't have anywhere else to go. I didn't have any other family and all my friends were at the party… except for Cricket. But I didn't want her to know… I didn't want *anyone else* to know. That only left one place. Somewhere nobody would ever think I'd go, which made it the perfect hiding spot tonight.

"Can I go home with you?"

CHAPTER 5

Georgia

H E SNORT-LAUGHED, BUT WHEN HE REALIZED I WAS
serious, the humor died, and I missed how beautiful
he looked when some of those harsh edges on his
handsome face smoothed out. But damn, was I grateful
I got to see it so close-up after all this time.

"Seriously? You wanna come to my house?" he asked.

"Yes. Please, Beau?"

"Jesus Christ. Fine."

He drove in silence for fifteen minutes before we
pulled up to his place. The difference in his side of town
and mine was vast. An addition when Mr. and Mrs.
Bradford had their fifth son made their house bigger and
the back half was newer. But on the front, the brick was
crumbling in areas, and the yard was in definite need of
some landscaping, unlike my gated community where
every single house was immaculate.

"You sure you wanna stay here?"

I turned in my seat and lifted my chin. "Yes."

"All right. Come on. Everyone should already be sleeping, so be quiet."

Following him inside, I was surprised to walk through a super-clean house down a long hallway to his bedroom. Nothing was on his walls except a bulletin board above a small wooden desk, and on it was a photo of him and his mother. My heart broke even more for him…

He dug through a dresser drawer and tossed a shirt on the bed. "Bathroom's just down the hall on the left. I'm gonna go check on my brothers and then use one of the others. Be right back." He vanished out of his door, and I scurried to the bathroom and scrubbed a little toothpaste over my teeth, used the toilet quickly, and then splashed cold water on my face.

I patted my face dry and leaned in and gazed at my reflection in the mirror, noting the swelling on my cheek for the first time. *Damn.* The mark reminded me of what my dad did to me, and my fingers started trembling.

He's been saving you for me.

I'm just getting started.

I knew now what this was all about; my father expected me to marry Tad. When I asked him why I had to go to the dance with a guy I didn't even like, he'd said it was the start of my new life, but I didn't realize exactly what he meant. Or maybe I did, but I just wouldn't allow myself to accept it. If I was forced to marry Tad, what that sick bastard did to me tonight was just the beginning of my miserable life. And I refused to live like that. I just had to figure out how to get away from him.

I'd start tomorrow, because tonight, I was safe.

Taking several long, deep breaths, I swallowed air until the acid cleared from my throat.

When I arrived back in Beau's room, he still wasn't in there, so I slid my shorts down and took my shirt and bra off, replacing it with his oversized tee that I forgot to take with me to the bathroom. I flinched at the pain in my side and lifted the soft cotton up to smell it, but the bruising on my ribs caught my eye. I turned my body to examine it in the mirror attached to Beau's dresser.

"What the fuck is that from?" His voice made me jump, but I didn't move away. I was too transfixed by the way the bruising seemed to darken by the second.

"He punched me here, too."

"Jesus." He kicked off his boots, and his footsteps were quiet and then faded away to nothing. I just stood there, staring at my battered body and wondering how the hell my night ended up like this. Never in a million years would I have thought Tad would attack me like he did. We weren't really friends, but we had been friendly. Our fathers golfed together, and he'd been to my house for family dinners. Something obviously happened between our families that I hadn't been told about yet, but still, I never imagined he'd turn violent.

Even if my father believed me, he'd probably blame me and definitely wouldn't do anything about it. If I had any strength left in me, I'd have laughed at the fact that Holt wouldn't give the first shit about his daughter almost being raped. It wasn't funny, so far from it, but at this point in my life, if I *didn't* laugh about it, I'd just cry. And I was sick of crying.

The door clicked shut, and Beau came to stand beside me. He took off his shirt and jeans somewhere along the way and wore only a pair of flannel pajama pants now. His big, strong body so close made me feel safe, and I wished things could have been different. I really did. Our eyes locked in the mirror, and he held up a wadded-up towel. "Ice."

I wrapped my fingers around the lip of the dresser with one hand and stood in an uncomfortable position with the other slightly raised so it wasn't covering the bruise. He knelt next to me and pressed the cold towel against the ugly purplish-red skin. A hiss of pain unexpectantly left me, and he grabbed my hand and set it on his shoulder for balance so I wasn't standing so awkwardly. "Shit. Sorry. It'll get better with the ice."

His skin was so warm. His whole chest and both arms were defined and sexy. Powerful.

It should have felt weird for me to be standing there in his tee and my underwear while he was shirtless, but it wasn't. It was like every other time he'd been close; all I wanted to do was be even closer.

His features softened, and the horrible things I'd said to him, the lies I'd spewed, pounded against my already aching skull. How could this guy who I'd been so mean to be so kind to me right now? When I laughed in his face and demeaned him, he still came to my defense. He gave me a ride to safety. And when he realized that my house was just as dangerous as that party and I begged him to let me come with him, he brought me into his home, where nobody would hurt me.

Tears rolled down my cheeks no matter how hard I tried to conceal them, and his brows drew together. He stood perfectly still as he took care of me, and I wrapped my arms around him so he wouldn't leave me. If this was the only chance I'd ever get to be this close to him, I was taking my shot, otherwise I'd regret it for the rest of my life. I pulled him tight to me and heard the ice pack fall to the ground, the cubes clattering on the hardwood floor. And then I cried in his arms, and he patted me on the back cautiously, which was way better than him pushing me away like I thought he would.

When that made me sob even harder, he inhaled a deep breath and held me tighter, rocking me back and forth soothingly. Not saying anything but just being there, as if he knew exactly what I needed... *again.*

He probably thought I was crying because of Tad, but I wasn't. It was because of him, because of Beau. It was always about Beau. I hated myself for how I treated him all these years. For how good it felt to be with him. How right it felt to be held by him. And how much time was wasted pretending to hate the only guy I had ever truly wanted.

And I knew it was time to tell him what he wouldn't let me say earlier.

"I'm sorry, Beau. I'm so, so sorry."

"Hey. Hey, it's fine."

"No, it's not." I untangled my arms and stepped back,

violently wiping away my tears. "I was so mean to you, and you're being nice to me for no reason."

He huffed out a laugh. "Oh, trust me. There's a reason, Georgia."

Confused, I pushed through his response because he needed to understand how deeply I regretted everything I had ever said to him that was mean or hurtful. And *why*. "I wasn't lying, Beau. My dad heard about us at the Pig and laid into me as soon as I walked in the door. God, he was so terrifying, and if your family's name was even *mentioned* after that night, his face would get all red and smoke would practically come out of his ears." I hiccuped out a breath. "He talked so badly about you but I *knew* you. The real you. And didn't believe any of the lies he was spewing about you and your family." The next part was hard, but I forced the words out. "I was afraid of him so I stayed away from you... for both of our sake. Then you got in trouble with the cops, and it made it even worse. And... and all of that aside, it was just safer to be mean to you and push you away than it was to confess how I really felt, how I really feel."

He held me at arm's length, searching my face. "He hurt you?"

"He did."

A realization came over him, and his shoulders sagged as his face scrunched like he was in pain. "Fuck, how did I not see that?"

"Because I didn't want you to."

His tongue swept across his lips, and he swallowed. "How *do* you really feel?"

"I… I…." God, this was crazy. "If it wasn't for him, I would have kept my promise—"

"You what?" he growled softly. I jerked in his arms, but he pulled me closer and lowered his voice. "Say that again."

"Come on, Beau. You have to know that."

His head shook in disagreement. "No, I don't. I thought you hated me and I didn't know why. I thought you were using your dad as an excuse. It's been killing me for years not to know what I did to make you hate me but all along you were telling me the truth." He blew out an angry breath. "Dammit. You've got to be kidding me. All you had to do was give me any sign that you felt the same and I'd have stopped teasing you, but it was the only way I could get you to acknowledge my existence. You barely even looked at me unless I pissed you off."

My lips rolled, and he watched, his fingers twitching against me, the sharp sensation telling me I wasn't dreaming and this was really happening. "I didn't know what my dad was capable of and I wouldn't risk him hurting you."

"I can protect myself. You should have told me."

I tilted my head and waited until his eyes came back to mine. "You told me you saw how I really felt by how I looked at you."

A slow, sexy smirk adorned his face, bringing back the cocky Beau Bradford that I knew. "Yeah. I did say that, didn't I?"

"You did."

"You were right," I whispered.

"I know I was, Gigi."

I bit my lip, but couldn't hold back an unexpected yawn, even as I tried to cover it by looking down.

He tilted my chin up and rubbed his thumb along my jaw. "You're tired." He moved aside and angled his head at the bed. "And you've had a rough night. Let's get some sleep and we can talk about all of this in the morning. Go hop in. I'll sleep on the floor."

"No, I will."

"You're crazy if you think I'm gonna let you sleep on the floor, Georgia."

A wild idea came to mind, but I didn't know if he'd go for it. "What if you sleep with me?" He raised an eyebrow, and I covered my face, laughing. "That's not what I meant. I mean… God, this is embarrassing."

"Hey." He pried my hands away and watched as he laced our fingers together. "You don't ever have to be embarrassed around me, okay?"

It was so easy to believe him. "Okay."

"I'm just gonna get this out there, and then you can decide what you want to do. Tonight, you were assaulted, and I don't want me being in the same bed as you to make you uncomfortable." I tried to talk, but he lifted a finger and covered my lips. "I also don't want you to worry that I would ever, ever hurt you in any way, or do something that you weren't a hundred percent on board with. I promise you, Gigi, I will never harm you. Ever. My dad probably won't care since I'm eighteen and all, but even if he's mad, I'll deal. So if you want me in that bed with you, that's where I'll be."

Listening to him talk about how much he cared about me made my insides all gooey. And that was why, with no hesitation, I doubled down. "I want you in that bed with me."

I loved the immediate grin of satisfaction that formed on his lips. "If you change your mind, just tell me."

"I won't."

Being with Beau was amazing. Laughing with him was wonderous. But doing those things in his bed was indescribable. I never thought I would be here, and now that I was, I didn't want to leave. We'd just been lying there, whispering in the dark, confessing secrets and making truth of the lies. His fingers would ghost over my skin every once in a while, and we'd hold hands, but otherwise, he'd been an absolute gentleman.

Just as I knew he would.

He reached over and turned on the lamp on his nightstand and a soft glow illuminated the room. "Don't look at me." I giggled and tried to duck my head, but he lifted my face with his palm beneath my chin.

"You're beautiful. I'm sick of talking to you and not seeing your face."

"I'm not wearing any makeup."

He rubbed his lips together. "Like I said, you're

beautiful. I've always thought that. Even when you had braces and a perm."

I rolled my eyes. "Don't remind me." He brushed my hair over my shoulder and I whispered, "I don't ever want you to think that I actually believe any of that stuff I said to you or any of the crap my father tried to put into my head."

"I don't. I mean, I did sometimes, but then I'd see you watching me when you thought I wasn't looking. I wasn't a thousand percent positive what it was, but I knew the way you reacted when I got near you wasn't because of fear."

"No, it wasn't," I whispered.

"Come here."

He pulled me down to him, and I laid with my head on his chest as his fingers stroked through my hair. I swore I was living a dream right now, one that I had been certain would never come true. I could barely keep my eyes open, but I refused to fall asleep because I didn't want to miss a minute of this.

"What do you want to happen here, Georgia?"

I want this to last forever.

"Tonight?"

"No. That's not what I'm asking. No matter what happens, we'll always have tonight." He kissed the top of my head, but I felt that declaration in my heart. "I'm talking about tomorrow, the day after, the week after. The *future*. What do you want to happen with us in the future?"

If he only knew. I wasn't ready to tell him about Tad. I angled my head up, and he did the opposite so he could see me. "I'm not sure." I didn't even know what was planned for my future, but whatever it is, I only wanted it if Beau was with me.

Hurt bounced around in his eyes, and he pressed his lips together, clearly disappointed in my answer.

"I want to be with you, and I have for a long time, you know that." I added quickly. "But I don't know how with my dad..." I trailed off, leaving the rest up for interpretation. I didn't want to say the words, but I didn't have to because he knew.

He smiled and rubbed his thumb across my lips. "Can I tell you a secret?"

"Yes."

"You're almost eighteen. You can be with whoever you choose. But I don't want to make anything difficult for you, so just tell me what you need from me, and I'll do it. If I have to wait for you, I'll wait. Hell, I've wished and waited for this moment to happen forever, so it doesn't make a difference if I have to hold off a while longer. I have all the time in the world as long as I know you feel the same way I do, and that in the end, we'll be together."

"We will be." I just had to figure out how to get out from under my father's thumb, and I only had a couple of months until I could do that. Then yes, I wanted to be with Beau forever. Snuggling even deeper, my lashes fluttered closed and let the strong beat of his heart lull me to sleep.

CHAPTER 6

Beau

THE FOLLOWING MORNING, GEORGIA WALKED INTO the kitchen in my T-shirt, tied at the hem in a knot at her waist with one of my flannels over the top, and the shorts she wore the night before. Her eyes widened at the sight of me, my four brothers, and our dad sitting around the table eating breakfast. She stopped in her tracks, and the five other guys at the table froze mid bite and just stared at her.

Partly because she was Georgia Westbury, mostly because she was in our house, and definitely because she came out of my room. But fortunately, they knew better than to give her the third degree.

"Hey, Georgia. You hungry?" I asked between bites.

"Uh…"

I kicked out the chair next to me, but she didn't move. "Y'all, this is Georgia. Gigi, my brothers and our pops. Pancakes are almost gone. If you want one, you better get over here now."

She lifted an arm and wiggled her fingers, muttering a hello as she skirted around the table and sat next to me, subtly scooting her chair closer. I loved that. I loved being the guy she looked to for comfort and safety. Shyly, she folded her hands in her lap and fiddled with her fingers. Everyone stared at her with angry scowls as they took in the slight bruising on her cheek.

"Son," my father grumbled between gritted teeth.

"I took care of it, Dad," I assured him as I reached behind me to grab a plate and then placed it in front of her.

"You better have," he warned. Even though I already told him everything that happened and why she spent the night, he still felt the need to make sure I dealt with the reason she had a bruise on her face. He wasn't concerned in the least that a girl was in my bed because he trusted me, but I was still kind of surprised he didn't even blink when she walked in the kitchen. "Eat up, young lady." He tossed a pancake her way.

She jumped at the sound of the cake landing on her plate, but smiled when my dad winked at her and then poured her some juice from the carton sitting in the middle of the table. "Thank you, Mr. Bradford."

"Wade, darlin'." He winked at her.

The boys all looked at me when she was buttering and pouring syrup on her pancake, asking silently what in the hell was happening, but I just shook my head. I'd tell them later. I purposely didn't let them know she was here because if I did, they'd act weird. I figured the shock factor was my best bet.

And I was right. They were too stunned to be jerks or embarrassing about it.

After a couple of minutes, conversation resumed, and Georgia relaxed and started eating. "These are really good."

"Thanks," I replied.

Her lips parted in surprise. "You made them?"

"Yeah." I did all the cooking for my family.

"When did you get up? I didn't even hear you."

"Been up a couple of hours now."

She stared at me in disbelief. "It's only seven thirty."

"I always get up early."

"Don't be modest now, boy." Dad cleared his throat and folded his napkin on his plate. "Beau here's a great cook. Wakes up early every mornin' to make sure we've all got full stomachs before we start the day."

"Dad," I mumbled, not wanting him to embarrass me further.

"Everyone pitches in. We had to after..." He sniffled, then cleared his throat, and the entire room filled with a rush of sadness that was palpable. "Beau's in charge of the food around here. Brody does the dishes. Brock does the laundry. Bear cleans the house, and Baker takes care of the outside." He winked at the last statement, and we all chuckled, knowing damn well the outside of our house looked like shit. Dad failed to mention that he worked fourteen-hour days and did the grocery shopping.

"I can't keep it nice like Mommy," Baker's innocent

66

voice made everyone look his way. "But we're going to get some flowers today to try."

Georgia blinked her tears away. "I'm sure you'll pick out some very pretty flowers, and it'll look absolutely beautiful."

Baker smiled a toothy smile, the sight something I haven't seen on him in a while. "Do you want to come with?" he asked, his boyishly soft, unsure tone making my chest constrict. "Since you're a girl, you can help me get the prettiest ones."

Georgia glanced at me, and I shrugged, letting her know it was okay if she wanted to come with but also not to feel pressured. "Of course. I'd love to."

"Really? Wow, thanks. I'm gonna go get dressed!" He slammed his chair in and the dishes on the table shook. "I have pictures from a magazine. Let me go find them." Then he practically threw his plate into the sink before he rushed down the hall.

"Well, I have some work to do before we head out. Nice meeting you, little lady."

"Yeah, you, too, Wade."

My brothers disappeared from the table one by one, and after Georgia and I finished eating and put our plates in the sink, I grabbed her hand and led her to my room. I still couldn't even believe she was here. "You don't have to come if you don't want to. I know you've probably got better things to do than gardening with the Bradfords on your Sunday."

"I want to. I just need to run home and change

clothes." She picked at my shirt and bit her lip out of embarrassment.

"I can take you if you want."

"Really? I was going to ask Cheyenne since she lives close, but if you want to, that would be great."

"Sure. Let's go."

I walked her through the kitchen but stopped when we reached the threshold. "Shit. Forgot my wallet. I'll be right back." I rushed down the hall and swiped it off my dresser, and when I got back, I heard Brody talking to her from the living room. "I swear to Christ if you're just doin' this to fuck with him, I'll—"

"*Seriously*?" I snapped at my brother and watched Georgia's shoulders sag in relief. "I leave her for thirty seconds, and you pull this shit? You have a problem, you talk to me."

He glared at me, not regretful at all. "You know where I'm coming from, Beau."

"I don't care where you're coming from. If you ever talk to her like that again, I swear I'll break your goddamn jaw."

He shrugged unapologetically, then went back to watching TV, his brotherly duty fulfilled. I linked her pinky with mine, then shot him a look that said this wasn't over.

I grabbed my keys off the hook and led us to my truck. "Sorry about that."

"It's fine. At least he cares." Her soft smile, and the way she rolled with the punches wasn't something I was expecting out of her. Nor was I thinking she'd wake up feeling the same way she did last night. The part of me that always thought she was too good for me was worried she'd run out the door and never look back. But by some miracle that hadn't happened, and knowing it wasn't a fluke was so damn awesome. Made me feel like a million bucks. "What?" she whispered.

"Nothing… I just…" I tucked a strand of hair behind her ear. "I've never seen you like this before."

"Like what?"

"I dunno." I shrugged. "Nice."

She punched me playfully in the shoulder. "Shut up. I was always nice. It was you who's a jerk to me and then made me be not-so-nice."

"Only because you were a bitch to me." I backed out of the driveway and headed toward her house.

"Don't call me a bitch."

I gave her a sideways glance. "Well, what would *you* call it?"

The good of the past twelve hours crashed in the blink of an eye, and she crossed her arms protectively. "How about we don't call it anything and just stop talking about it?"

"Okay, okay." I held my hands up in surrender. "I'm sorry, I was just joking."

"I know, but I don't want to be reminded of how awful I was to you, and I don't want you to keep remembering."

"It's all forgotten, okay?"

She flattened her lips together and nodded.

To solidify my point, I reached across the bench seat and took her hand, rubbing my thumb over the pulse point in her wrist. Our short drive down Main Street and up the hill to her house with no traffic put us there in almost exactly fifteen minutes. Before I turned onto her street, I pulled over. "Are you going to be okay if your parents see you driving with me?"

"No." She shook her head, and the honesty of her answer stung. "My mom would be okay, but you know my dad wouldn't. They're not home, though, so it's fine. She left this morning to visit her sister, and he golfs every Sunday morning, so he'll be gone."

"All right," I muttered, trying like hell not to be offended as I pulled into the long driveway and stopped at the gate.

"Punch in four, seven, eight, six, two."

Before I typed in the code, I raised a brow. "You're trusting me with the code? Aren't you afraid I'll use it to break into your house and steal all your worldly possessions?"

"You're such a jerk." She huffed with a smile, and I reached over to put the code in. She unbuckled her belt when I came to a stop at the front door. "You wanna come in?"

"Nah, I'll just wait in here." The last thing I wanted was her dad to find out and have me arrested for trespassing or something.

"Be right back."

I leaned over to push her door open, then she crawled

down. I turned the radio up while she was changing and only heard two songs before she ran out in a pair of cut-offs and a pink tank top with her hair up in a ponytail. She was slow to get into her seat, and when she sat down and buckled, I found myself unable to look away, which was nothing new. But this time, she was so close I could see the little specks in her eyes.

"What?"

"Nothing. You're just really pretty." She had put on a little makeup, but only enough to accentuate her natural beauty. The red mark on her cheek was still there, and it pissed me off every time I caught sight of it.

"Thanks." Her teeth sank into her lip, and she fought a smile. She gazed out the window, and I wanted to kick myself for how stupid I sounded. "I just have to say…" She turned in her seat, and I glanced at her out of the corner of my eyes. "I'm really sorry for what I said to you that day in the bathroom. It's seriously been haunting me, and I need you to know that I didn't mean it."

"I thought we weren't talking about it anymore."

I turned the volume on the radio down so I could hear her better.

"We're not. At least after this. I just had to say it. I chickened out before, so I just needed to get it out."

My lips quirked into a half smile. "I notice that's how you work. You've gotta build up your confidence and go over shit in your head before you say what you're feeling."

She didn't disagree. "So then please, let me say it."

"Don't sweat it. It's fine. I was a dick. I deserved it."

"But you're not," she insisted.

"Not what?"

"A dick."

I snickered. "Yeah, I am."

"No, you're not. After what an idiot I was last night, what you did for me with Tad was not something that a dick would do."

"One, you weren't an idiot. You didn't do anything wrong, so don't you dare blame yourself for him attacking you. Tad's just an entitled prick who needs to have his ass kicked. And two, any decent guy would do what I did."

She rolled her window down, and the breeze hit her hair, the long locks flying around the cabin and infusing her sweet scent of strawberries into the air. It kind of ticked me off I didn't have a camera so I could take a picture of this moment and always have it to look back on

"Why'd you come up there in the first place?" she asked curiously.

I cleared my throat. "You didn't deserve the way I snapped at you outside on the porch. I felt like shit for it, so I went inside to try to find you. Cheyenne said she saw you go upstairs, so…"

She leaned over and kissed my cheek, then rested her head on my shoulder. "Thank you, Beau. I don't even want to imagine what would have happened if you weren't there."

"You don't have to worry about that anymore. He touched you once, but there won't be an opportunity for a second time. I can promise you that." The desire to keep beating his ass last night was strong, and at that point, she was still technically considered my enemy. But now that she was mine? There's no telling how far I'd go to protect her from him... or anybody. "And I never said thank you, either, but it means a lot that you'd come to me to say sorry about my mom."

"I really am sorry."

"Thanks," I gritted out.

"Has it been... I mean, I know it's been hard, but how are your brothers doing? Your dad?"

I took such a deep breath it burned my lungs. "It's definitely been a rough few months since she passed. Mom was the glue. And now she's gone, just like that."

She squeezed my forearm. "I can't imagine."

"My dad shut down and left me to deal with everything. I didn't get time to grieve, really. Instead, I kept the house running. I got my brothers fed, their clothes washed, and to and from school every day. I was the only one who stepped up." I told her. "But after over a month of only getting three hours of sleep a night, I had enough and told my brothers they needed to pitch in."

"How did they react?" she asked.

"They grumbled about it at first but eventually came around. And once things around the house got better, my dad did as well. At least they had been for the past couple of weeks. I think him seeing us living our lives made it safe for him to push forward and keep going when all he wanted to do was stop."

"That's amazing of you, Beau."

I shook my head. "It's not, I just did what I had to."

"I hope it's okay that I say your mom raised such a great guy. You took care of your family when they needed you, and you took care of me last night. She'd be proud of you."

I blinked away the burning in my eyes and felt a sense of pride I hadn't in a really long time. Our lives would never be the same, but we were all trying as best as we could. And now, having Georgia, she made it better and finally gave me a reason to look forward to something.

CHAPTER 7

Beau

BAKER WAITED ANXIOUSLY OUTSIDE WHEN I PULLED up. He clumsily jumped up into the truck and crawled over me so he was squeezed in the middle. "Everyone else is coming," he rushed to say as he pulled the seat belt over his lap. "Dad said to wait, and you can follow him."

"All right." I laughed, loving how at ease my baby brother was.

"Here, I found the pictures. Which ones do you like the best?" He basically forgot I was there, and turned his back to me and handed Georgia the pieces of a magazine he'd ripped out. "My mom always had pink and purple, but since it's just us guys now, I think we need the orange ones. Do they make blue flowers?"

Georgia giggled and shuffled through the papers. "I'm pretty sure flowers come in every color you can think of. We can probably do a little bit of everything."

"Okay!"

Dad came out and gave a little smile when he saw Baker happily chatting away. I drove behind him to a large garden center in Lawless while my brothers made faces at us the whole ride. After we spent a couple of hours there picking out flowers and all sorts of shit for the yard, we got burgers for lunch at a little diner called Rusty Rooster.

"Sit with me, Georgia!" Baker exclaimed as he grabbed her hand and pulled her toward a booth. We couldn't all fit in one, so we had to split up, and my dad and the other three took a seat at a nearby table.

"Whoa there, bud. You can't steal my girl." I joked as he tried to have her sit next to him.

I wrapped my fingers around her arm and playfully pulled her away from Baker, but he put up a fight. After a couple of rounds of tug-of-war, I won when I reached over and tickled him.

"Hey, that's cheating!" He laughed, frantically pushing my hands away.

"I know." I ruffled his hair and slid in first, loving that Georgia had a smile pulling on her lips.

"I'm going to get two scoops of ice cream with sprinkles after we eat lunch," Baker stated without looking at the menu. "And a burger and fries, but I have to have water because ice cream has a lot of sugar." He pouted.

Georgia made a cute little face, scrunching her nose. "You're right. There is a lot of sugar in ice cream."

"That's why it's so good."

"Right again. What flavors are you going to get?" she asked.

"I don't know yet. I'll decide after I eat my burger," Baker replied. "Do you like hamburgers?"

"I do, but I get cheese and extra pickles."

He stuck his tongue out. "Gross. I don't like pickles."

"Do you like cucumbers?"

"If I can dip them in ranch," he said.

"You know pickles are cucumbers, right?"

"No way!"

She nodded. "And raisins are grapes."

"What else?"

"Let's see… peanut butter is peanuts. Applesauce is just apples mushed up. Chocolate milk comes from brown cows." She couldn't help the little grin that pulled at her lips, giving away the joke.

"You're lying. I almost believed you, too." Baker laughed as he bounced on the cushy vinyl, then jumped out. "I need to pee."

"Use your manners in front of a lady, son." Dad scolded him as he passed, but he was already down in the little hallway that led to the bathrooms, so I'm not sure he even heard him.

"Thank you for coming," I nudged Georgia with my elbow. "Baker's having the best time, and it's really good to see him so happy."

"You don't have to thank me. I should be thanking you because I'm having the best time, too."

I tucked some hair behind her ear and wanted so badly to kiss her, but when I looked over her shoulder

77

my brothers were all making kissy faces. I subtly slid my hand behind her back and flipped them off.

"Boys," Dad barked, and we all went back to our best behavior.

Georgia fit right in with my family, joking around and laughing with them like she'd grown up with us. I loved her sitting next to me and rubbing her leg against mine when she moved, her hair tickling my arm. It was like she was just meant to be at my side, and as corny as it sounded, I never wanted her to leave. It made me realize just how much I missed her.

Lunch was great, and after that one incident, my brothers didn't do anything else to embarrass me.

We headed back and worked outside for the rest of the afternoon. While Georgia and Baker planted flowers, the rest of us cleaned up the dead leaves and made the yard presentable. "Do you still have a mom?" We all froze in the middle of what we were doing when Baker asked Georgia that.

"I do."

"I don't anymore. She's in heaven because she died. Do you think she's watching us right now?"

I gripped the rake in my hand and felt a splinter slice through my palm, but the pain didn't register.

"I think so. I think she's an angel, and I also think that if you ever need to talk to her, she'll be there to listen. She won't be able to talk back, but sometimes just talking to someone is all you need to feel better. And she might be in heaven, but she'll always be your mom, and she'll always want to listen to you."

"She can hear me?" Baker asked in awe.

Her eyes were frantic as she searched for me, and I nodded. "Yeah, buddy. She can."

"Cool." He stuck his tongue out and went back to digging in the dirt. "I'll talk to her later. I'm busy now."

"Thank you," I mouthed to her, and she gave me the smallest smile before joining Baker.

Georgia was surprisingly good at gardening and didn't give a crap that her white shirt was covered in dirt, and as the sun set, we all stood in front of the house and admired our handiwork.

"Well, your mother would be proud, boys."

"Yeah, she would." Brody wrapped his arm around Dad, and Baker copied him by doing the same to his other side.

"Do you think she would think it's pretty like hers were?" my baby bro asked with so much apprehension that I cleared my throat and looked away.

Georgia grabbed my hand and gave a reassuring squeeze. Her touch sent a calmness through me, and I pulled her closer and tucked her into my side, where we fit together like two pieces to a puzzle.

"Yes, Baker. She'd think they're absolutely perfect," I promised.

"Good." The relief on his face let me know that maybe things really would be okay.

"Why don't you all go and get washed up?" Dad

ANNA BROOKS

suggested. "I'll clean this, and we'll order some pizzas for supper. How does that sound?" He was getting choked up, and we all knew it, so we agreed and left him to have some time alone. And I was grateful I didn't have to cook for a change.

Once in the house, Georgia went to the bathroom first so she could clean up, then I met her in my room while my brothers did their own thing. She was sitting on my bed with a pillow in her lap and set it aside as soon as I entered. "Is he going to be okay?"

Of course, she didn't miss the intensity of everything that just happened with Baker; hell. Hell, she was paramount to today being what it was. I closed the door behind me. "Yeah, it happens every once in a while, but it's been a couple of weeks since the last time. I'm sure it'll never stop."

"No, I don't suppose it ever will." She twirled her thumbs almost nervously. "I had fun today."

"Me, too."

"I like planting flowers. Whenever we had gardeners come to the house, I always watched them, and they were nice enough to teach me what they were doing. One day, my dad came home when I was helping them, and he lost his mind. Fired them on the spot and then made me take a shower because he said a lady should never be dirty." She rolled her lips together. "There have been so many little things like that throughout my life that I always just... ignored. Or maybe I was in denial. But when he got physical after he saw us together, I couldn't deny

80

it any longer." She sighed. "I haven't put my hands in dirt since then, but I'm glad I did today, so thank you for giving me that."

I rubbed her back while I ground my teeth thinking about her being treated that way, especially in her own home where she was supposed to be safest. Something she loved being taken away from her...her flesh and blood hurting her like that—made me feel a helpless rage unlike anything I'd ever felt before. But it took seeing her sitting on my bed, so vulnerable, to know me getting pissed wouldn't help anything. She didn't tell me that for me to get angry because she'd had enough volatility to last a lifetime. She told me because she trusted me and was grateful for what we shared today. And I was proud to be the guy who made her happy. I wanted to tell her that she could plant flowers every day, drag mud into the house, and kiss me with dirt on her face, and I wouldn't care as long as we were together. But I figured that was too much too soon. So I just said, "You're welcome, Gigi."

"I don't get it."

"Don't get what?" I asked in confusion.

"Why my dad warned me away from you. Y'all are the nicest group of guys I've ever been around, and it baffles me that he acts like you're not good enough."

That definitely stung, but I powered through. "I'm not sure why some people do what they do."

"Me either."

"Remember last year during the pep rally when

Austin Donovan ripped his clothes off and ran around the gym in his underwear?"

She giggled. "Didn't he paint his chest?"

"Yeah. And he got suspended for it but when he came back everyone thought he was the shit."

"I don't know why, that was *so dumb*." She snorted.

"My point is, I guess when you're not worried about consequences you don't care about much." I lifted a shoulder. "I have to do good in school, and I had to be in clubs because if I wanted to go to college, I needed to have the best application I could to even get in, let alone get a scholarship. Dad can't afford to send five kids to college, and if we jeopardized our education now, it effects our entire future."

Her eyebrows were pulled together as she listened to me talk. "I never thought about that before."

"I know."

"What are you going to do... about college?" she asked hesitantly.

"I don't know. I need to be around to help my dad, so I guess I'm going to figure it out after the summer. But probably will just go somewhere local once the boys are all back in school this fall."

Her beautiful features softened. "You're such a good son, and the best brother those boys could ask for. I hope they know how lucky they are to have you."

"We love each other, but I don't know that any of us would consider ourselves lucky right now."

"I get that, but you'd all be wrong," she insisted. "Y'all

might think I'm lucky, but I'd give anything to have the kind of family you do. That's worth so much more than money."

"That's what all the rich people say." I grinned.

She rolled her eyes. "Seriously, your family is awesome."

"They're all right."

"No, they're the best."

"*You're* the best. The way you were with Baker today was…" I had to think of the right words. "It means the world to me that you handled him the way you did. Not a lot of girls would care so much."

"Good thing I'm not like a lot of girls."

I cupped her chin and ran my thumb across her cheek. "No, you're not."

She leaned her face into my palm, then took a breath. "I think I should go."

"What? Why?"

"I just… I need to shower, and I think after today, your family needs you. And I don't want to be in the way of that."

"You're not."

She took hold of my wrist. "I'm glad you think that, and it's really been amazing being with you and your family. I can't even tell you how happy I am that we're okay again, but—"

"But what?"

"I like you, Beau. I always have. I want this to work

more than you know," She bit her lip shyly. "But I need to be careful... for both of us."

I knew she was still worried about her dad, and I got it, but hearing the words meant a hell of a lot, and it was all I needed. For now, at least. "I understand. And for the record, I like you, too."

"I know." She looked down and sighed. "I don't want to, but I need to go home so things are as normal as possible right now. I don't want him to have the upper hand when I turn eighteen and tell him we're together. He won't be able to control me anymore, but until then..."

Her voice began to shake and the fear taking hold of her put my nerves on edge. "What aren't you telling me, Gigi?"

"Beau, he's... he's not a good man. We didn't touch on it much last night, and the flower thing was just the tip of the iceberg. My father is a *monster*. I mean, what kind of dad forces their daughter to go to a dance with a guy she hates?"

"About that... you and Tad were never a thing, right?" I hated seeing them at prom so much that I had to walk away so I wouldn't kick his ass for being so close to her.

"God, no. If I ever was with him, it was because my dad made me. And if he seriously expects... Nope." Her head rocked back and forth, and before I was able to ask what he expected, she went on. "If I had it my way, I'd rub it in his face right now, but that would be reckless. I'll be a legal adult in just a couple of months, so I need to be smart until then. We'll have to keep our feelings for each other to ourselves for a while until I can get out from under his thumb."

I hated that it had to be like this, but I understood it. It was a small town, and word traveled fast. If this was better for her, then I was all for it. "I get it, but just for the record, I want you here. I don't want you to go." I loved waking up with her hair all over my pillow and scent on my sheets. I wanted to do that every day, but if it wasn't safe for her, then I'd just have to wait until it was. Once she was eighteen, she was free to make her own decisions.

Her grip on my arm tightened. "I don't want to either, but I haven't been home since this morning when I changed. I need to at least be seen by my dad when he gets back later."

"Are you going to tell him what Tad did to you?"

"No! I—I don't want to tell anybody. The less attention I have on me right now, the better. And we both know that he won't get in trouble for it anyway."

I had to respect her wishes, but unfortunately, she wasn't wrong. "All right."

"When he's gone on business, I'll be here, and when he's home, I'll work on how I can be with you. I can come back tomorrow, though… if you want."

"Yes, I want. But tomorrow's Monday, so I work." Dammit.

"When will you be home?"

"I'm at the garage seven until three."

She glided her soft hands up my arms and wrapped

them around the back of my neck. "Then I'll figure out a way to be here at three, waiting for you."

I dropped my head and kissed her. I couldn't resist anymore. And the moment I claimed her lips, the cool calmness around me crashed, and hungry desire overpowered me. For years, I wanted this, *needed* it, and it was even better than I remembered. But she wasn't close enough. I grabbed her ass in one hand and the back of her head with the other and plastered her to me, not wanting even air to fit between us. She succumbed to the domination of my lips and parted her own, allowing my tongue access to explore. To taste. To vow with my mouth what I couldn't with words.

Yeah, this was more than I thought it would be. *Finally.* And what I imagined was pretty fuckin' powerful. Her lips were soft, and she tasted like heaven. And when she made these little noises in the back of her throat, I felt it in my dick.

It was fucking perfect, but it was too much. I needed to stop before it went too far, because our first time wouldn't be in my bed with my family in the other room. And definitely not right after she was attacked. I wanted to take my time exploring every inch of her hot body. I wanted it to be special, just like she was. Reluctantly, I pulled back and dropped my forehead to hers, both of us breathless. Her lashes rested on her cheeks, and when they slowly rose, and her glistening blue eyes found my own, I asked, "Tomorrow?"

"Yeah." She breathed the word and touched her fingers to her lip. "Tomorrow."

"Good. Let's go, I'll take you home."

When she got into my truck this time, she slid in the middle and rested her head on my shoulder for the entire drive. I let her off in front of the gate by her house, after we made out for a little bit. By the time I got back home, everyone was in the living room watching a movie.

"Pizza will be here soon!"

"Cool." I laughed at Baker's enthusiasm and tossed my keys on the kitchen counter before joining my family, quickly realizing Georgia was right. We all wanted that security of being together, even if none of us said it out loud. After we ate, Baker came to sit next to me on the floor. I threw my arm around his shoulders, and he relaxed into me. He had become subtly needy, and if she was there, I would have had her next to me so he wouldn't have gotten the opportunity to do this and get the comfort he needed.

The movie we watched had a sequel, so we put that on next. It was about halfway through when a pair of red and blue lights flashed against the white curtain in the living room. I sat up, and even though I knew my dad and brothers were all here, I still looked around in panic to make sure.

"What on earth?" Dad stood and began to walk to the door just as there was a knock.

More like pounding, actually. "Police! Open up."

And it hit me why they were here before I even saw them. Shit. "*Dad.*" With one look at me and the regret on my face, he paused and dropped his head, realizing what I told him earlier that morning was the reason they were there.

"I know, son. I know. It'll be okay."

Taking a deep breath, he turned the knob and opened the door, and I looked over at my brothers. "I'll be back soon, okay? Just please take care of each other and don't let Dad do something stupid."

"What's going on?" Baker asked, pushing to his feet.

I lifted my chin at Brody. "Watch him."

He nodded and grabbed our little brother and put his arms around him just in time for me to hear my name being called. "You're under arrest for the assault of Tad Clancy."

CHAPTER 8

Georgia

I WASN'T ASHAMED TO BE SEEN AT THE BRADFORDS' house, but until I wasn't under my father's control any longer, I wouldn't risk him finding out. He came home late last night and left this morning for a trip. I didn't know when he would return, but the last thing I needed was for him to find out about Beau through somebody else, so I had to be careful even when he was out of town. It was risky letting Beau drop me off, so I would have to think of something else next time.

My mom trusted me, but she still cared about where I was and who I was with, so when I'd lied and told her I was going to hang out with Cheyenne tonight, she asked, "Is her dad going to be there?"

"Yeah, he always is."

"Well, okay. Then have fun. How is she doing? I haven't seen her in a while."

Yeah, because I never want to be here, let alone bring a friend home because I hate my father. "She's good. Excited that school is done so we want to spend as much time together as we can before she starts her classes this fall."

"Gosh… I can't believe you've graduated. Time goes by so fast."

"I don't know. It feels like it's taken forever to be done with school."

She pressed her lips together. "I remember feeling that way, too, when I was younger. But the older you get, the faster it goes, so Georgia, I want you to listen to me." She held my arms and looked into my eyes. "The next couple of months, until you're eighteen with no responsibility, I want you to enjoy every moment while you can."

That was cryptic. "Mom…are you okay?"

"I'm good. Just promise me you'll have a blast this summer. Be safe, but have as much fun as possible. I trust you to make good choices, so as long as you check in with me daily, you don't have to worry about me saying you can't hang out with your friends."

Guilt began to creep in, but my desire to spend more time with Beau outweighed any responsibility I felt for telling her the truth. "Okay, thanks. And I will enjoy my summer." I hugged her and waited outside for Cheyenne to pick me up, then she dropped me off at Beau's like we'd previously arranged. Being my best friend, she didn't hesitate, and I trusted her to keep things between us… and lie to my mom if need be. But it didn't sound like that would happen.

As soon as I said goodbye to her, I skipped up to the front door, excited to see Beau, even though it had been less than a day since we'd been together. I had to talk myself out of coming here earlier because he was at work, but I literally counted down the minutes until he said he'd be home. If it was anyone but him, I would have been surprised that my feelings were so strong, but I'd had a crush on him my whole life. And even though we'd had our rocky times throughout high school, now that the air had been cleared, it was just… *easy* between us. It was natural, Beau and me, and I only wished we could have been together longer.

I was still about ten minutes early, so I was surprised to see his truck here already. But surprised in a good way, hoping that maybe he was just as excited to see me so he came home from work early. Before I knocked, I smoothed down my shorts and flicked my hair back over my shoulders. The door was opened almost immediately, and before Wade could utter a word, I knew something was wrong. The somber look on his face said it all.

"What happened?" He motioned for me to come in. As soon as the door latched, I glanced around and didn't spot Beau, so I asked again. "What's wrong? Where is he?"

His brothers were all sitting around the kitchen table, heads down, bodies tense.

"Where is Beau?" I demanded in a panic. My purse and bag fell to the floor with a thump. Fingers clenched tight in a fist, I pressed it to my heart, terrified it was going to pound right out of my chest.

"He was arrested last night."

"What?"

Wade put a hand on my shoulder and bent his knees so he was at my level, and it reminded me so much of Beau and how he calmed me with just a look. There was no doubt Beau got so many good traits from his father. "Tad Clancy pressed charges and—"

I lurched forward. "I need to go. I have to fix it. I need—"

"He doesn't want you to." Baker spoke up, and I was so lost in my head that I didn't see him get up *or* feel him take hold of my hand, so when his voice sounded from next to me, I jolted in surprise. "He told Dad, and Dad told us, so it's our job to take care of you until he gets home. He's going to be back tonight, and you're just supposed to wait for him."

I looked up at Wade when he cleared his throat. "He doesn't want you doing anything because you told him you don't want anyone to know about... *what really happened.*"

He was being discreet for Baker's sake, and despite wanting to yell from the rooftops that Tad tried to rape me, I gathered my composure enough not to frighten the kid. "But I will. I'll tell them if it'll get Beau out of there and his name cleared."

"That's sweet, but I'm afraid I have to insist you just wait for him here," Wade said gruffly. "If you go down there, that'll just upset him and the situation more. I'll be getting a call soon to let me know what time I can get him to bail him out, so until then, why don't you just make yourself at home, okay?"

My stomach was in my throat, and I shuffled back until I hit the wall. My vision was blurry, and my ears were echoing loud, staticky white noise.

"Baker, look through the cupboards and find something for us to eat. Georgia, come sit down. I'll get you some water." I was snapped back to reality when Brody gently tugged on my wrist, and again, I jerked in surprise because I didn't notice him so close either. "Come on."

Brody smiled and angled his head down at Baker, who was still holding my hand and clearly confused and scared about what was happening. "Okay. Yeah... fine. But how about I make y'all something to eat tonight?"

"You can cook?" Brody feigned shock.

I glared at him, and he winked, and just like that, I felt like I was a part of this family again. I was still scared for Beau, but the support of his brothers was reassuring. I rummaged through the cupboards and found it pretty empty except for a huge box of granola bars, some chips, and a couple of empty sleeves of cookies. Baker told me nobody really ate since breakfast, probably because everyone was so worried, so I wasn't sure if I was making an early supper or a late lunch. Either way, it would be enough to fill their bellies. The shelf with the canned items was relatively full with a ridiculous amount of peanut butter hiding almost everything else, so I dug around and found two different brands of pasta sauce and several boxes of macaroni noodles.

Grabbing those, I prayed there was cheese in the fridge and was pleased when I found exactly what I was looking for. Baker helped me grate the cheese while the other brothers hung out, playing cards and talking at the kitchen table.

After mixing all the ingredients, I popped a version of baked ziti in the oven and started doing the dishes. "That's my job. I'll do them after we eat." Brody reached over me and shut the water off.

"It's fine. I didn't mind, really. I need to do something to keep myself busy right now anyway."

"I get it, but I can't let you do them alone. Beau would kill me."

Shrugging, I flipped the tap back on and handed him the bowl I was rinsing. "Suit yourself."

Brody took it from me and laughed. "Listen, I need to say sorry for how I acted yesterday."

"No, you don't."

"I do. But you have to know that once I got to high school, I saw how you treated him."

He did. I remember Beau being ahead of me in the lunch line, but I didn't know that Brody was ahead of him. When I asked if they had more cake, the lunch lady told me that Beau had gotten the last piece. Since he was still close, he heard my question and set the dessert on my tray. The tray that I then took to the trash and dumped the contents. *"I wouldn't take food from you if you were the last guy on earth."* And worse than Brody witnessing all that was seeing the hurt on Beau's face when I tore him to shreds.

"I know you did, and I'm so sorry. I didn't mean any of it."

"He's the best, so the last thing I was gonna do was sit by and watch some girl he's liked for years finally give him the time of day only to break his heart."

The news that Beau actually liked me was not something I didn't know. However, to find out his family knew how he felt about me made the wound even deeper and on the verge of irreparable.

With a smaller house, way more people but only one parent, and less income, I felt more at home here than I did in my own house. That was sad. But the honest truth was money didn't buy happiness, and it didn't matter that I never wanted for anything when the only thing I needed was love and security. And I'd never truly had that... until last night.

I knew what my dad was capable of, and I knew that Tad's father was dirty. What I couldn't comprehend was how Henry Clancy still had any authority in this town since his toxic history was public knowledge. Look at what had already happened with Beau—I knew it was Tad's doing. This was not a good sign, and I was absolutely terrified of what other *messages* would be sent once I told my dad about Beau.

"I don't want to break his heart, and I won't," I reassured Brody. Because the truth was, I'd do anything for him.

"Good."

"Why is she doing the dishes?"

I expelled a huge sigh of relief I'd been holding since I got here when I heard that deep, calming voice.

Turning around with soapy hands, I found Beau in the same clothes he wore yesterday, looking handsome as ever but tired as hell.

"Beau!" Baker jumped down and ran to him, throwing himself at his big brother. "You're home!"

"How did you get here?" Wade bellowed from the living room. "You were supposed to call."

Beau's normally bright eyes were flat, and he flashed a regretful smile as he hugged Baker. "I walked, Pop." Then he asked again, "Why is she doing dishes, Brody?"

"I wanted to." The timer cut through my daze, and I quickly wiped my hands with a towel and turned my back to him as I grabbed a potholder and opened the oven. I needed to get the food out before it burned, and if I stood there and stared at him any longer, that's what would happen.

"You cooked, too?"

I set the baked pasta in the middle of the table, and it was like I wasn't even there and Beau didn't just walk in after being in jail all night. Even Wade came and sat down, scooping a huge portion on his plate.

"Come here," Beau whispered the words as he walked toward me, crooking a finger.

I'd go anywhere he wanted, do anything he asked.

Meeting him as fast as I could at the mouth of the hallway, he took my hand and tugged me behind him until we were in his room where he shoved the door closed and then yanked me so hard against him that I slammed into his chest. He buried his face in my neck and wrapped his arms around my waist and held me so tight it was as if I was wearing a corset.

The emotion I held back in front of Baker cracked, and I allowed a couple of tears to roll down my cheeks before I slid my hands into Beau's thick brown hair. I waited until I gathered my composure and gave a gentle tug, and he lifted enough to look into my eyes. "What happened?"

"Nothing you need to worry about."

"Beau, seriously." I tried to pull away from him, but he didn't let me go. "You were arrested because of me."

He shrugged. "Not because of you. And it's not surprising that Tad stooped to this level. He's just a punk-ass bitch who will never learn, and unfortunately, right now, he's unable to be stopped."

"I know, and that's exactly what scares me." He couldn't argue that and dropped his forehead to mine. "I'll tell them what he was doing to me and that you were protecting me. That you saved me from him."

Beau rolled his head back and forth. "It won't work. He has witnesses to corroborate that you and he left before me, and I followed y'all out. His story is that I was jealous you two were together and attacked him."

The warmth from his embrace began to seep out of me, and bitter cold went straight to my bones. "He what?"

"Yeah. He paid me a visit. Said he saw me bring you home yesterday. He dropped the charges, but this was my warning to stay away from you."

"He can't do that."

"His dad is powerful, so that's where you're wrong.

But listen, whatever shit he's trying to prove is between him and me now. It's not even about you. Just stay away from him and if you see him somewhere, leave." He blew out a rough breath. "I understand why you didn't want to go to the cops that night, and it wouldn't even matter now since he made sure to get his story on record first. But eventually, he'll fuck up, and I plan on being there when he does. Because when that finally happens, I'm gonna get back at him for hurting you."

There were so many fears I had, so many worries. And so many questions I needed the answers to. The biggest one was what if this was all Beau and I will ever have. How would I survive without him? But when he threatened doing something to Tad, I only managed to ask, "What do you mean—"

"There's hardly any food left, so if you wanted any, y'all better come and get it." I bit my lip when the amused voice of Baker interrupted us from outside the door, and Beau groaned.

And then he tilted his head and pressed his lips against mine. My eyes flew open at the shock and brilliance of him kissing me. His tongue barely touched mine before he pulled away and kissed my cheek, leaving me dazed. "I'm starved, Gigi. Let's go eat."

I put my worries on the back burner so he could get some food in his stomach, and then we watched a movie with his family, and when Wade walked out of the room halfway through, Beau followed. They both came back about ten minutes later, and I could tell Wade was pissed off at what they talked about.

I slept over that night, and he held me so tight in his arms, it was heaven. But it was also the real world, and he had responsibilities, so when he went to work, I walked to Cheyenne's house. She lived near him, and even though her dad made a lot of money, they never moved from their first house to a bigger one.

I snuck around to the back door that Cheyenne left unlocked for me and tiptoed through the kitchen. "Hey," I whispered as I kicked my shoes off inside her room.

She rolled over and rubbed the sleep out of her eyes. "What time is it?"

"Six forty-five."

"Too early." She groaned and rolled to her side.

I climbed in, got under the covers, and sighed, "I'm in love."

"Yeah, I can see that." She smiled and yawned at the same time. "You're glowing."

"He's the best, Shy."

"I'm so happy you're happy. I—"

She stopped talking when there was a knock on her door, and her dad stuck his head in. "Hey, Georgia. Cheyenne, I'm gonna take off for work. Thought I'd bring Chinese home for supper. Sound good?"

"Yeah. Can Gage come over, too?"

His prominent Adam's apple bobbed when he swallowed. "If you want."

"He's my boyfriend, Dad. Of course I want him to come and eat with us."

"Fine. But he can't come over until I get home, and he's gone by ten."

"Dad!" Cheyenne yelled. "I'm eighteen years old."

"My house, my rules, kid."

Shy glared at her father. I knew why he didn't like Gage. He was actually the kind of guy my dad accused Beau of being. Cheyenne was sweet, too sweet for him, but when I tried to talk to her about it, she just got defensive.

"Okay, Dad, fine. He'll be gone by ten."

"And he won't be in this room with the door shut, either."

"Whatever."

"Love you, Cheyenne." He smiled at me and then closed the door behind him.

She rolled back over to face me. "Sorry, he's so annoying."

"No, he's just being a dad. A good one."

"I know." She sighed. "Anyway, I'm hungry. Do you want to go to the Pig for breakfast?"

"Duh." I joked sarcastically. "Then do you mind running me home to get some clean clothes?"

"No problem."

We ate breakfast, then swam in my pool for a little while, and then Cheyenne dropped me off at Beau's again. I was waiting in his room when he got home from work, and he tackled me on the bed, and we made out for a while before he took a shower.

He was still responsible for the cooking, so whenever he was in the kitchen, I was too. That evening, miraculously, Beau and I were alone while we were making supper. Wade was still at work, and his brothers were all at the park playing football with a bunch of other kids. "Are you sure you don't want to go join them?" I asked as I was peeling potatoes. "I can finish this."

"No, Gigi. They're gonna need food when they get home, so I have to do this."

"But do you *want* to?"

He sighed and set his palms on the cutting board. "No. I'd rather not have this responsibility, but I do. It's life... my life. And I have to lead by example by showing my brothers that you don't always get to do everything you want when you have certain responsibilities. So next time Brock gets home late from hanging out with his friends and he's tired and doesn't want to do laundry, he'll learn that he either needs to stay up or not hang out with his friends so late, but either way, the laundry's gotta get done."

"But can't you do something to maybe... make it easier on you?"

"Like what?" he asked.

I shrugged. "I don't know, like a crock pot or something."

"I learned how to cook from watching my mom. We

ANNA BROOKS

don't own a crock pot. She always cooked every meal from scratch."

I made a mental note to go to the store. "How do you decide what to make?"

"I only cook the same like ten meals. They're all basic—spaghetti, pot roast, tuna casserole, tacos. Lunch is always sandwiches. And during the week, breakfast is cereal and fruit. I try to do pancakes or French toast on the weekends, though."

God, he was amazing. And he was going to make an amazing husband and father someday. He always managed to make me feel special with his words, and I had the opportunity to do the same for him, so I wasn't going to miss my chance. "You're incredible, Beau."

"I'm just doing my part."

"No." I set the peeler down and caressed his jaw with my fingertips. If it wasn't for the fact that he was trimming a raw chicken, I know he would have touched me, too. But this was the perfect opportunity for me to focus on him for a change. "You are amazing. You're selfless, you're caring, you're sweet, you're funny. And you love hard. I see the way you are with your family, and I know that whoever you end up with is going to be the luckiest woman in the world." *And I want it to be me.*

"Kiss me," he rasped.

I pushed up to my toes and ran my tongue across his lips, and somehow, he took over without even using his hands. It was so exhilarating. A preview of what life with

102

him would be like. It was what I wanted; *he* was who I wanted.

Almost every day for the next two months was more of the same, and it somehow got better. Not only being with a family who loved each other but knowing what I had to look forward to because I wasn't giving this up. Not for anything.

My birthday was just around the corner, and I couldn't wait for the proverbial shackles to get cut from my wrists. Cheyenne couldn't be my cover anymore because she was now working full time with her dad at his dental office and also going to school to become a dental hygienist, so I had to get creative. My friend Cricket lived above the Pickled Pig, so I asked her if I could park my car there, and without question, she said I could. If anyone saw it, they'd think I was with her, so I'd just do that for a few days until this could all finally be over.

Which was why I found myself walking down the street after parking at her apartment and headed to the garage where Beau was working. I wanted to surprise him and was practically skipping down the sidewalk when a familiar car pulled up and the window rolled down. My knees locked and my fingers trembled as revulsion coated my stomach. "Have you gotten my messages?" Tad asked.

He'd been calling me, but I refused to even listen to his voicemails or open his texts. If I pretended not to see his name flash across my phone screen, then I could pretend he didn't exist. "Nope."

"You have. What I want to know is why you haven't returned my calls."

I was petrified of him being so close, but I would not let him see my fear. "Are you seriously asking me that right now? I don't want anything to do with you after what you did to me." *And to Beau*, but I couldn't say that.

His lips pulled up into an evil sneer, and he leaned farther over the center counsel of his BMW. "I'm afraid you're not going to have a choice here very soon."

"Fuck off, Tad." I stormed away, and he threw the car in reverse and jumped on the curb, cutting me off. "Are you crazy?" I looked around and saw Mr. Hayes from Farm and Feed sitting in his truck at the stop sign across the street. "People can see you acting this way." But maybe that was for the better.

"Nobody's gonna do shit to me, Georgia. Now you go have your little fun but be warned, this isn't over."

I crossed my arms. "What's not over?"

"You and me."

"There is no you and me."

He laughed and shifted gears. "Keep telling yourself that." His tires screeched, and he sped forward, hitting the bottom of his bumper on the curb. "Oops. I guess I need to head down to Bradford and Sons to have them fix this. You want a ride?"

I shook my head and took that second to put on a blank expression. "What are you talking about?"

"You tell me."

"I'm done with this." I dropped my arms and turned around, heading back to Cricket's.

"You're going the wrong way."

I ignored him as he drove beside me, and when we got to the corner, he turned it sharply, almost hitting me as I crossed the street. I jumped back and ran into the brick wall of the drugstore, and leaned on it to get my bearings.

My fingers were shaking and my knees wobbly, but I refused to let him win. I wiped my sweaty palms on my shorts and blew out a breath, then continued toward the garage.

I made sure no one was around, then darted into the building and was greeted by Wade. "Hey, Georgia. Fancy seeing you here."

"Hi. Is Beau here?"

"He had to run to Lawless to pick up a part, but he should be back soon."

"Oh, okay... I'll just go then."

He waved his hand. "Nonsense. Stay here. He won't be gone long."

I glanced around nervously. "Can I go in the back or something?"

"Of course." He slid off the stool and I followed him through the door that led to the bays. He pushed open the office door. There was a desk, mini fridge, filing cabinet, a cabinet with a bunch of different keys, and a couch that he moved some newspapers off. "Sorry, it's a mess."

"That's okay."

"Well, there's some Coke in the fridge. Help yourself. As I said, Beau won't be gone long."

"Thank you."

He moved toward the bays but stopped and raised a brow as he took in my disheveled appearance. "Is everything okay, darlin'?"

"Sure, fine."

"It doesn't seem fine," he muttered.

I knew my cover was blown, so the words came pouring out. "Tad saw me on the way here and basically accused me of coming to see Beau. I just hate that it has to be this way, but we're so close to not having to worry about my... I don't know what all Beau told you, but my father is not a fan of your son."

Wade leaned on the doorjamb. "I know he's not. Which is why I think y'all are doing the right thing by making sure you're strong enough together, and that he has no legal hold on you, because when he finds out..."

"What?" My knees gave out, and my butt found the couch. "What do you mean? Do you know something?"

"No, darlin'. I just know what kind of man he is."

I should have been surprised, but I guess I didn't know any better when I was younger. Now that I was older, I was smart enough to recognize the way he was wasn't normal or okay. "I'm nothing like my father."

He dipped his chin and said firmly, "I know you're not."

"But I treated Beau so badly and—"

He cut me off in a firm yet kind tone. "I respect that

you did what you thought you had to to protect my boy. It's enough for me."

"Thank you, Wade."

"I'll let Beau know you're here." He pushed off the frame. "Let me know if you need anything… anytime, Georgia, you hear?"

I sank into the cushions when the door closed and ran my fingers through my hair. If Beau's father was anyone else, I wasn't so sure they'd be as understanding as Wade, but for whatever reason, he was, and I was so grateful.

It wasn't long before the door swung open, and Beau sauntered in. I'd never seen him in his coveralls, and he was so hot it left me speechless. He took hold of my hands and pulled me to my feet, then laid a hard, wet kiss on me before resting his forehead on mine. "Hi."

"Hi."

His hands moved down to my waist and held me close. "Best delivery ever."

"What?"

"Pops said I had a delivery in the office." He kissed my nose. "Best delivery ever." I held my breath, waiting for him to say something about what I told Wade about Tad, but he didn't. "You ready to get out of here? If we leave now, we can have the house to ourselves for a bit."

My teeth sank into my lip, and my belly fluttered. "I'm ready."

He trailed a finger around my belly, slid his palm down, and then cupped me, making my toes curl. I gasped and held his shoulders. "Yeah, you are."

I was. I was so ready for him. Not only physically, but emotionally too. More than anything, I wanted a life with him. I just had to get through the obstacle of my father first, then it would be smooth sailing. Because Wade was right. I did what I did to protect Beau, and once my dad found out, I'd give it all up, risk everything for love. I'd take the hurt if it meant Beau didn't have to.

CHAPTER 9

Georgia

"**A**REN'T YOU HUNGRY?" MY MOM ASKED AFTER I sat picking at my salmon for ten minutes.

"Not really." My stomach was churning because I was fearful of what was about to happen. I didn't know I was going to do this tonight, but since my dad wasn't going to be here on my birthday tomorrow and we were all together tonight, I knew it was time. "I stopped and got a burger on my way home because I was starving."

"Why were you eating fast food? You know that's absolutely terrible for you."

I swallow tightly, then turned to address my dad. "I know, and now I'm paying for it because my stomach hurts from all the grease." Which was, of course, a lie.

"Told you so."

He was such an asshole. After being around Wade for the past couple of months and seeing how he loved and supported his kids, I realized just how terrible my father really was. I'd always felt disdain for him, but lately, it had turned into something pretty close to hate. "I know, Dad." I took a drink of water and then circled the rim of the glass with my finger. "Oh, I forgot to tell you my car's been acting funny."

"What's it doing?"

I shrugged. "I'm not sure. It's just making a weird sound. I was thinking of stopping at Bradford and Sons tomorrow to have them—"

"Absolutely not." He slammed his palm on the table. "Why?"

"Because I said so. I told you I don't want you anywhere near that boy or his trashy family."

While he was lecturing, I stole a glance at my mom to find her with her head down, but her hand was in such a tight fist around her fork that I wondered if she could bend it.

"I really don't think—"

"*It's not your place to think*!" He pounded his hand on the table, clattering the silverware. "Beau Bradford's a troublemaker, and I will not risk my daughter's safety with the likes of that boy. He's a felon, attacking poor Tad for no reason. In fact, you will stay away from that entire family and start spending more time with Tad. His father said he hasn't seen you around much this summer, and that's going to change."

"I've been hanging out with Cheyenne."

"She's gone. Tad is your only friend now, and soon, he will be more."

"Excuse me?"

"You heard me."

I didn't understand what he was going on about. "Do you even care that I don't like Tad, and he makes me uncomfortable, and that he—"

"No, I don't. I don't want to hear that nonsense. Tad is a fine boy from a respectable family."

Beau would never ever hurt me, but I knew I wouldn't be able to convince my dad of that, not that it made a difference. How... God, how was I supposed to do this? I was beginning to question my plan because even if I was eighteen, Tad and his family could make Beau's life miserable. My God, why hadn't I thought about this more? "The Bradfords are not trash, Dad, and that's a really mean thing to say. They run a successful garage and lost their wife and mother. Everyone in town goes to them to get their cars fixed, including you until recently. What did they do to make you hate them so much?"

Whenever my dad got mad, a vein in his forehead protruded. And right now, that sucker looked like it was about to explode. I had never talked back to him like this. "I don't need to give you a reason. If you want to keep your car, your money, and any chance you have at a decent future, then you stay away from the Bradfords, do you understand me?"

"No, I don't."

My mom gasped as my dad pushed away from the table, then before I even saw it coming, he backhanded me so hard the chair tipped, and I crashed to the floor.

"*Holt!*" Mom yelled as he stormed out of the room,

and while I was still seeing stars, she brushed my hair off my face and helped me sit up. "I'm sorry, Georgia. God, I'm so sorry."

I blinked a few times until things were clear and found her with tears streaming down her face. And despite myself, I smiled, almost glad he hit me. It only solidified that I was doing the right thing, and I needed to get away from him. "It's not your fault, Mom."

She shakily wiped the tears from beneath her eyes. "Yes, it is."

"It's not. He's just an asshole, and he always has been. All he cares about is money and what all the other rich people think about how much money he has. I hate him, and I'm done living here with him. He can take everything from me—I don't give a shit about any of it! All I care about is Beau!" I pushed myself to standing and rushed up to my room to grab my stuff. I had no clue if my dad left or if he went to his study, but I did not give that first fuck. I was leaving.

I ripped clothes from hangers and emptied my sock and underwear drawer. I shoved some shoes on top and zipped the duffel bag. I was just about finished putting my makeup into my purse when my mom came into my room. She closed my door. Great, that meant he hadn't left. So help me God if he tried to stop me, I'd die fighting him to get away. "Is this really what you want to do?"

"Yes. Hell, yes. What kind of father slaps their daughter across the face like that?"

She shook her head as if to clear it. "Where are you going?"

After I shoved the last of my necessities into my purse, I wet my lip. "I think you know where I'm going." There was no way she didn't with what I said at the table. Her lashes rested on her cheeks and another round of tears fell down her face, but she was smiling. It was scary. "*Mom.*"

"I love you, Georgia. Go. Be happy, for as long as you can." And then she turned around and walked out of my room, and I was left standing in a puddle of confusion.

But I didn't let it stop me for long because I was out the door and on the road to Beau's in about thirty seconds. It wasn't too late, so I knew everyone was still awake. I just hoped I could get by them without anyone noticing the redness on my cheek.

I parked in front of his house for the first time, not giving a shit who saw. I loved him, and I wanted to be with him. I didn't care if my dad took everything from me, and I was left penniless because Beau was all I needed.

They always left the front door unlocked until everyone was in bed, so I opened it and was so glad to see it was just Baker playing video games. "Hey, buddy."

"Hi, Gigi." He didn't even look up from his game, and I snuck by him, then opened Beau's door without knocking.

"What the fuck happened to your face?" Jumping up from his bed, he reached out to touch my cheek but held his hand back. "Who did that?"

The strength I had to get out of there wavered, and

113

I could feel my bottom lip quivering, the realization of my reality starting to hit me as the adrenaline wore off. "My dad."

"Motherfucker." He cupped the other side of my face and took my bags, tossing them on the floor somewhere.

"What happened?"

"I asked about you and—"

He dropped his hand and ripped open his door so hard the knob put a hole in the wall. I rushed to keep up with him and tried to stop him, but when I dug my nails into his forearm, he yanked it away. "Beau, stop."

"I'm gonna fuckin' kill him." He disappeared through the back door and had his ass in the driver's seat of his truck practically before I could blink. It was a miracle I was able to jump into the cab myself, but when I did, I began pleading with him.

"Stop, Beau. *Please*. He's not worth it."

I had never seen him so mad before, and I scooted over and put a hand on his thigh and the other on the back of his neck, resting my forehead on his jaw. "Please slow down. Pull over somewhere so we can talk. Please, Beau." I pleaded with him to no avail. "For me."

He hissed through his teeth, and ironically enough, we were right by the garage, so he pulled around back and parked among a bunch of other vehicles, most of them in the same kind of beat-up shape as his truck was. His hands loosened their grip and fell to his lap, and he dropped his head to the steering wheel.

I ran my fingers through the hair on the back of his

head and waited for a cue from him on how to proceed from here. I had no idea what was going to happen next. I didn't even know if he'd let me stay with him, but all I knew was I couldn't go back home.

"Was that the first time he hit you?"

It wasn't the first time he put his hands on me, but I wasn't going to add more fuel to the fire. "Yes."

His leg bounced, and he cursed. "I feel so fuckin' weak."

"*What*?"

"I can't do anything, Gigi. As much as I want to and as badly as I want to go over there and beat the living hell out of him, *I can't*. I don't know how to protect you from him. Or Tad. My hands are tied right now, but one day, I'll make him pay. I promise you that." He hissed out a breath. "I don't know how or when, but I will. I just have to be smart about it, so it'll take some time, but if I have you through it, then it'll all work out. We'll be okay, right?"

"Yes, we will. We have each other, and we'll be fine."

He turned to face me and pushed me down so I was lying on the bench, one of his feet was planted on the floorboard and the other leg was bent beneath him. "I won't let him win. Either of them." His hands roamed my body, over my shirt, just beneath it, his fingers trailing beneath the waistband of my shorts.

"It's not quite midnight yet."

"Close enough," I whispered. And I couldn't wait any longer. I knew he was waiting for me to tell him I was ready, and I was. "Take it." I couldn't think of a better way to bring in adulthood.

His head snapped back, and his nostrils flared. Beau held himself over me, his muscular arms caging me in as his hands gently cradled my face. "Are you sure?"

Losing my virginity in the cab of his truck outside the garage wasn't on the top one thousand ways I thought it would happen. But it was the only way I wanted it because it was him and me. It was *us*. I had never wished for anything more in my life as much as I wanted him to be my first. I don't know how it happened over the past couple of months, but I had become obsessed with him. I was infatuated by his strength, his charisma, his charm. He was gorgeous inside and out, and I needed him to make me his in a way nobody else ever had or ever would.

"Yes." I opened my eyes and found him so close our lashes brushed. "I want you."

"Then that's what you'll get." He rubbed his nose along mine. "But not here. Not like this."

"It's okay..."

He jerked his head. "It's not. And I have this big plan for tomorrow, so we'll have to wait until then."

"What plan?"

"I took time off work, and want to take you to a hotel in Lawless so we can spend the day together celebrating your birthday. I want to spend the night there and really be able to—"

I pushed him off me and sat up. "Let's go."

"*Now?*"

"Yes. Now. I want to wake up there on my birthday with you."

"But I'm not ready. I need to go pack the food and get you your present and—"

"I don't care about any of that." I pushed out a breath. "I mean, I care, but I just want to be with you. We can order room service and eat out of the vending machine and just have it be us. I want that more than anything." God, no worrying about anyone or anything sounded like the best gift ever. Getting away from this town sounded perfect.

That night, which started out so incredibly awful, turned into one of the best of my life when I gave him all of me.

"Are you sure you're ready?" he asked.

We were both naked, and he'd already given me an orgasm with his mouth and gotten me as ready as he could with his fingers. At first, I was nervous, but very quickly he made me think of nothing but his hands and lips, his strong body on top of mine as he kissed me into oblivion.

"I'm more than ready." I whispered, cupping his jaw.

He reached between us and I felt the silky smooth tip of his cock rub against me. It was nice, different than his fingers, and I wanted more. "Tell me if you need me to stop."

"How can I do that if you never start?"

His eyes smiled, but his lips were still a straight line. "Just promise you'll tell me."

"You could never hurt me, Beau."

117

He swallowed, then pressed inside. I gasped at how much he stretched me, and he pulled out. "Are you okay?"

"Yes. More."

Again, I only got a little bit of him because I squirmed, and he must have thought it was because of pain. "Sorry, Gigi."

"It doesn't hurt."

His eyes searched my face. "It doesn't?"

"No. Please." I wrapped my legs around his thighs and sat up so my lips were by his ear. My arms went around his back, and I clenched his hair and his firm ass. "Fuck me, Beau."

His chest rumbled, and he thrust his hips, his glutes tightening under my hand. There was a sharp twinge of pain, but it only lasted a second and then all I felt was him. Inside me. "Fuck," he murmured, and I tightened all of my limbs when he pulled back. "I'm not leaving you, Georgia. Never gonna leave you." Another thrust and I couldn't hold on anymore.

I fell to my back, and he stared deep into my eyes as he moved inside me. His chest was damp, his abs flexed, and when he lowered himself, his biceps bulged. The power behind him made my stomach flutter. It was unlike anything I'd ever experienced, and I let the pleasure overtake me.

My back arched, and my breath hitched as my orgasm built. "Beau," I moaned, afraid of everything I was feeling.

He untangled my fingers from the sheets and wound

our hands together, pressing them into the mattress. "I've got you, baby. Just let go. I've got you. Always."

My body flew into another dimension as sheer, unadultered bliss washed over me, and I squeezed my fingers around his and my nails dug into his skin so hard he bled. And he didn't pull away. It didn't even phase him that I was hurting him, because he groaned as he thrust once more and climaxed. But still, he didn't move his hands.

Devotion sank deep in my soul, down to the marrow of my bones, because he was *letting me* hurt him to bring myself pleasure, to make it good for me… whatever I needed, no matter how it affected him. I always thought it, but there was no question now more than ever that he'd sacrifice himself for me. And as much as I loved it, a part of me was scared for just how much he'd endure to ensure my well-being.

CHAPTER 10

Georgia

"Okay, Mom. I will. Yeah, love you, too. Bye." I flipped my cell closed after ending the quick conversation I just had and stared at the ceiling.

Beau called my name and waited until he had my attention. "Is everything okay?"

"Yeah. My dad left this morning for a conference, so she asked me to come home tonight so we could talk."

"Do you want to?"

I tossed my phone on the nightstand and rolled over. We were still in the hotel, and spent all morning in bed, cuddling and talking. I was kind of sore from last night but in the best way possible. It reminded me of what we shared, and it made my heart burst.

"I mean, no. I'd rather be with you, but I need to tell my mom everything. Plus, I need to go get more of my stuff. I don't really have a place for all my clothes, but I'll keep them in my trunk or something, at least until he takes my car away." Because as soon as he found out about Beau, I knew he would take more than my car.

"Just keep your stuff at my place," he told me. "I can clear out more space in my closet."

"That's sweet, but I need to put on my big girl pants and get a job and an apartment and—"

"You live with me. You don't need to get an apartment."

I licked my lips and dreaded saying this, but it was the truth. "Beau, come on. That's sweet, but I can't stay the—"

"Yes, you can."

"I love that you want me to, and I do, too. But realistically, I can't. There are already six dudes in your house, and I need a job, and I do want to go to college." I'd actually gotten an acceptance letter and everything, but then my dad told me I had to stay here another year before I went with no explanation.

I think I was so used to him being such a controlling bastard that I didn't even realize how much he manipulated my life. I was and still am young. I didn't know any better. So when he told me something, I listened. I didn't have any other choices until very recently.

"We can get a place together."

I loved that idea. "Are you serious?"

He shrugged like he didn't just rock my world in the best way. "Yeah. As long as it's close to my family so I can still help. I've gotta move out eventually, and now that I'm working full time at the shop, I make enough money to pay for the rent, so why not? I mean, I won't ever be able to give you the kind of life you have now, but—"

"You give me more, Beau." I got choked up even talking to him about it because the intensity of everything that had happened between us the past couple of months had hit me like a tornado. Fast and destructive, parts of me torn to shreds while some pieces were left standing, untouched and saved from catastrophe. "Money doesn't matter. I swear to God I couldn't care less about designer bags or big houses. I'd be happy on the street as long as I was with you."

"Let's not get hasty, now," he joked, and I laughed right along with him. "In all seriousness, I'd rather struggle together than have it easy without you."

How did I get so lucky? "You really want to tie yourself to me? I still don't know how my dad is going to react and—"

"I don't care about your father. You're eighteen now, Gigi. He can't control you anymore. You don't have to be afraid of him."

"Okay."

When Beau usually smiled, it was just a sexy smirk. But right then, it was so big I saw his pearly white teeth. "This'll be awesome. God, I can't wait to start the rest of my life with you."

"Me either." I blushed as I bit my lip, thinking about how perfect it would be living with him. How great having my own space would be where I didn't get told what to do all the time by someone who didn't even care about me. I was unsure of my future, stuck between a rock and a hard place, and more than a little confused... but Beau made everything seem so simple. Like we could just be together, and everything would work itself out. And God, I prayed he was right. "Actually, I need to just go home now. The sooner I get there, the sooner I can pack and talk to my mom and then get back to you."

"Sounds like a plan, babe."

We left the hotel in the same clothes we arrived in, and he took me to the Rusty Rooster for a late breakfast on the way back to Warrenville. It was so nice, being out in public with him and not having to worry about who would see.

He linked our pinky fingers together when he pulled up in front of my house. No point in hiding it anymore. "See you soon." I giggled as he shook them vigorously and then held my neck, rubbing his thumb across my jaw. "You'll come to me tonight? And then we'll start our life together. Nobody else matters. Just me and you."

"Yeah. Just me and you."

"I love you. You know that, right?"

My mouth slammed shut, and I let his words sink in and memorized every syllable as warmth washed through me. "I do now."

"Good. Now kiss me and then go talk to your mom, and I'll see you in a couple of hours."

"It might take me longer than that."

"Six o'clock. Then I'm gonna take you out for an actual birthday dinner to celebrate."

God, I loved him. "Okay."

"Happy Birthday."

"You've already told me like ten times today."

He winked. "The day's not over, so expect to hear it again."

I grinned and then kissed him before I jumped down and walked down my driveway on cloud nine. I pressed the code for the garage and ducked under the door as it was rolling up. He was still watching, and I wiggled my fingers, and he pulled away.

"Now I know where you've been hiding."

The voice came from behind me, and I jumped and twirled around, dropping my purse at the sound of Tad's voice. "What are you doing here?"

"I knew I was right." He shook his head and leaned against the hood of my car. "Beau? Of all the lowlife pieces of—"

"He is not a lowlife, Tad. That'd be you. How the hell did you get in here?"

An evil sneer formed on his lips. "Does Daddy know you're spreadin' your legs for the town loser?" I ground my teeth together, and he laughed. "He doesn't. But I'll tell you what. I'm gonna get Beau's seconds anyway, so why don't you bend over right here…" He patted the hood of my car. "And let me get a taste of what I can look forward to after tonight? If I like what I get, then maybe I won't let him know you're ruining your family name for the entire town to see. Hmm?"

"You're sick. And I don't know what the hell you're talking about. You're never going to get any part of me."

"Oh yeah, I am, my little Georgia peach. I'm gonna have every sweet inch of you." He straightened his spine, and I backed up, searching for a way out. "So soon I can practically taste it."

"If you touch me, I'll scream. I swear I will, Tad."

"Nobody's around to hear you, so go ahead. But know this. You open your mouth, I open mine, and you really won't like what comes out of it. So unless you want Daddy knowin' your dirty little secret, I suggest you keep your mouth shut."

I couldn't care less what my dad thought of me anymore. I didn't need him or his money. I'd been happier with Beau and peanut butter sandwiches than I ever had been my entire life with cash and caviar.

I held my shoulders back. "Go ahead. Tell him, tell everyone. Beau and I are going to move in together, so the whole town will know, too and then maybe you'll finally leave me the hell alone."

Tad tilted his head, grinned, then tilted it in the other direction. "Nah… I actually think I'd rather keep that between us for now. I don't want our relationship to be jeopardized when my father hears you're used-up goods."

"We don't have a relationship, and we never will."

"You really don't know, do you?" he taunted.

Instead of giving in and being a pawn in this dumbass game of his, I grabbed my purse and stuck my hand inside so I could get to my phone. "Are you done yet? I have things to do."

"Sure. For now." He scrutinized me as he took a step backward. But before I could breathe a sigh of relief, he halted his movement and rushed at me, grabbing my arm. "I lied. One more thing. Please, I want that motherfucker to come at me again, but this time, I won't drop the charges. By all means, do tell Beau about this."

I struggled to get out of his grip, but he was hurting my arm so badly that all I could do was put my effort into trying to pry his fingers off me. "Tell him about what?"

His pupils dilated, I'd seen that look before, and before my feet had time to catch up with my brain, Tad's hand was covering my mouth. I didn't see it, but I sure felt his fist colliding with my head, and a sheen of black tinted my vision as I heard Tad laugh. "Tell him about this, bitch."

I heard my mom calling me, but she sounded like she was downstairs. Why wouldn't she just come up to my room? She knew I was packing my stuff.

"Oh my God! Georgia, baby, are you awake?" Dizzying pressure in my head alleviated when I was rolled over to my side.

"Ow."

The garage door shutting made my brain throb. "Please, honey. Talk to me. Are you okay? Do I need to take you to the hospital?"

Why would I need to go to the hospital? "I'm fine." I mumbled the words, or at least I thought I did.

"Can you sit up?" I wasn't left with a choice when she grabbed me by the shoulders and hauled me up. "Good job. Now stand up and help me get you inside. Come on, you can do it."

I summoned the strength to help her, and together, we grunted and groaned our way to the living room, where she set me on the couch. "I'll be back. Let me get you some ice." It felt like an eternity before I heard her again. "Here, hold this on your head."

She lifted my hand and pressed it against the towel. I hissed when it was lifted to my temple.

"I saw Tad driving away. Was it him? He did this, didn't he?"

At his name, it all came back. "Yeah," I whispered as the grogginess faded, and I became more alert. The reality of what happened, the sheer terror of knowing Tad had it out for me worse than I thought. That he wants Beau to see me like this so he'll retaliate.

"I knew it. That little fucking shit... just like his father. Your father. All of them. Rich, entitled, dickhead asshats."

I had never heard my mom swear so much, and I couldn't help when my lips twitched.

"Don't laugh, honey. Your lip is split. We don't need it to get worse."

I wasn't sure how much time passed, but it was enough for the ice to melt and for her to replenish it. I had taken a couple of painkillers and felt much better physically. Mentally, I was broken beyond repair, my heart shattered to dust. The light at the end of the tunnel was now a dark and winding road with no end in sight.

As we were sitting there, I told her everything.

About Beau, about what had transpired with Tad at the party, about how Beau had saved me and how close we'd gotten over the past few months. Then I told her about spending my birthday with him and what we talked about this morning. And she listened intently to all of it without saying a word.

For a minute, I thought she was going to tell me how stupid I was for seeing him, how disappointed she was in me for lying to her, but what she said next was something I never expected to hear.

"Do you remember yesterday when I said it was my fault?"

I rolled my neck to get the knots out of it, but it only made it worse. "Yeah, I do."

"Well… I wasn't lying. But considering the circumstances, I think it's best you know the truth so you can make the most informed decision."

"The truth about what?"

A smirk tickled her lips. "About how Wade Bradford and I used to be madly in love."

"*What*?" My entire body jerked as I sat up abruptly, and I winced at the throbbing pain in my head.

Mom sighed before she continued reminiscing. "We were young. Younger than you and Beau. But I gather from the way you feel about him that it was the same way I felt about Wade."

"I love him."

"I know you do, honey. I also know you haven't been staying with your friends because I saw you with his family at the garden store a while ago."

I dropped the towel with ice onto the floor since it was almost melted again. "I thought you were with Aunt Sue."

"I was going to be, but the day before I was supposed to be there, the night of the dinner party, she got sick with the flu and told me it would be better if I didn't come. So instead of staying home, I hate to admit I got a hotel in Lawless that morning and stayed there since your father was home. I was just enjoying the day and about to go into that burger place for some food when I spotted you. God, you were the happiest I had ever seen you. It reminded me of me a long time ago."

I knew that I was totally out of it because Tad punched me in the side of the head, but I wasn't sure I was actually hearing what she was saying. "You and Beau's dad?"

"Yeah, until *my* dad found out. If I had it my way, I'd have run off into the sunset with Wade and married him and had his babies. But since I was the only heiress of Stilen Oils, my father literally locked me in my room until I turned eighteen, then forced me to marry your father because they needed to knock out a competitor, and the only way that could be done was with collateral. They needed the security of our families being legally bound together to guarantee one or the other didn't do anything to jeopardize the deal. I never graduated from high school, and I have no skills. I'm merely a tool to be used whenever I'm needed."

"No."

She smiled sadly. "I had a maid sneak birth control pills to me because I did not want a child born into the life I was forced into, but your father found them. I paid for that dearly, and he got his way nine months later. I do not regret having you. Not for a single second. But I do regret not being a better mother. I only wish I could have given you the life you deserved."

The ice was long gone, and my body was so heated listening to her that I felt the water at my feet start to boil. "You did give me a good life, Mom. I was happy. You always made sure of it even when he was hurting you, too. But why can't you do that now? Why don't you just divorce him?" I knew... I swear I always knew something was up with her. My mother tried her best to love me, but it never felt completely right. Like we always had some invisible wall between us, and I never understood it. Until now.

"Oh honey, you don't know what they're capable of."

I laughed and then sucked in a breath through my nose as a sharp pain shot through my ribs.

"Sorry, bad choice of words. You need to know something else. I wanted you to have your summer with Beau, but now that you're eighteen, we need to talk." Her breath hitched. "I'm so sorry, Georgia. I'm so, so sorry."

"About what?"

"Your father owes Judge Clancy a favor. And you're a smart girl, so I know you know what it is."

My stomach was already queasy, but I actually dry heaved. "Tad?"

"Yes."

"He's going to force me to marry him? He can't do that!" I cried.

"He's going to try, but he doesn't know what I do."

"Apparently, I don't either," I snapped. "How could you know this and not tell me?"

She took my hands in hers. "Because I've been preparing."

"What did you do?"

"As soon as he found out about you and Beau kissing, I knew it was going to end worse than I thought, so I started—"

The garage door opening echoed, and she snapped her jaw closed. Both of us surveyed the kitchen, waiting for him to walk through, my palms sweaty and her fingers wrapped tight around mine.

"He's not supposed to be home yet. Shit. Don't say a word, Georgia. Let me do the talking, you hear? It's time I finally put an end to this."

My dad rounded the corner, looking royally pissed off and ready to take that anger out on someone.

But Mom didn't let him. No. She jumped up and stood in front of me, but to the side so she could point at me. More accurately, so she could point at my bruised-up face and neck. "You choose right now, Holt. I swear to God."

My dad actually came to a stop when he saw me. The harsh lines on his face were still there but the edge to his bright green eyes was soft as he looked me over... something I'd never seen before. "Who did that to you?"

Why did he care? It's not like he'd never left marks on my body.

"The man you were going to force her to marry to get yourself out of debt." She reached out and took my hand when he lurched forward. "Yeah, I know everything."

My father's face paled, and his mouth opened and closed like a fish.

She panted and clenched her fists like her life depended on it. "I know that you're a selfish, egotistical, pompous man, but you are far from stupid. What you don't know is I have a secret account that can make this all go away."

His eyes perked up.

"Yeah, and I'll do it, Holt, for her. If you don't agree to my terms, I'll empty my accounts, and you'll be screwed." I had no clue what she was talking about, but apparently he did, because the color drained completely from his face as panic enveloped the room. "So right now, what's going to happen is I'm packing up my daughter's things and taking her to college. I'm staying with her until she heals and gets her new life set up. Then I'll come back and I'll help you deal with Clancy with the stipulation that Tad never contacts her again. You ruined my life, and I've let you ruin hers for far too long. This ends now."

My father, the man whose blood was running through my veins, didn't speak another word. His fixed stare and clenched jaw said it all. He shook his head, then turned around, and a second later, the door to the garage slammed shut.

"What just happened?"

"Like I was saying, I knew what he had planned and outsmarted him. I got your books and tuition taken care of. I found you a cute little apartment close to the campus. I'm giving you a chance to go make something of yourself. To get you out of here."

"But Beau's here."

She sat next to me. "I know. And if you want to stay and try to make it work with him, there's not much I can do for you, Georgia. The Clancys will feel slighted no matter what, but if they see y'all together, there's no telling what they'll do. We just have to hope the money I've got to give them is enough to get them off your back."

The thought of Beau getting thrown behind bars because of me, of his family getting unfairly targeted, of Wade's business getting shut down were too much. Mom was right. I had to go. For him. It was the only thought on my mind as I packed my clothes while she grabbed my social security card and birth certificate out of the safe. She put all of my medical records and a stack of pictures in separate envelopes and shoved them into a bag.

By the time my car was loaded, I could barely stay

awake, but Mom wouldn't let me sleep. "Just a little longer, honey. I need to pack a cooler. Stay with me for a half an hour and then I'll get you out of here."

I sat on one of the stools by the island and realized what was happening. It didn't feel real. Everything that I ever wanted was in the palm of my hand, but fate came in and slapped it out before I could even close my fingers around it. "Mom, I can't leave him."

"You have to, Georgia. At least for a little while." She closed the fridge and set a couple of bottles of water in a small cooler. "Pretend you're just going off to college like a normal kid. You'll see him again, let this all blow over."

"What if it never does?"

She swallowed. "It might not. But all we can do is hope."

"I know, but I don't want to. I love him." I sobbed, my throat closing and my chest so tight it hurt to breathe. "This isn't fair."

"I know it's not, and I'm sorry, but it has to be this way for a little while. Everything is ready. I have maps, hotels booked, and now the cooler." I sat up on the couch and rubbed the sleep out of my eyes, realizing this was actually happening. And it was happening *now*. "Do you want to at least say goodbye to him before we go?"

"No!" I practically screamed and she rushed toward me, taking my hands. "Mom, I need to just get out of here. If he… if he sees me like this, he'll do something he can't take back. He'll wind up in jail and that cannot happen. He cannot find out."

She pressed her lips together. "He loves you."

"He does. Promise, Mom, he can't know the truth. Promise me he'll never find out what hap—" There was a knock on the door as the bell rang. I'd recognize Beau's silhouette anywhere. "Mom. Promise me." I panicked and started to stand.

"Okay, okay. I promise." She grabbed my arm and helped pull me up, then shuffled me right around the corner. "Don't move." And then I listened as she lied to the love of my life about the reason I left him.

CHAPTER 11

Bea

Present day

"**H**EY, MAN, YOU HEADED OUT TO THE TAP?"
I scooted out from underneath the hood of Suzy Hayes's car I was working on and wiped my hands on a worn-out rag. "I dunno. I've been here since eight. Thinkin' about just heading home." Putting in twelve hours at the shop on my day off wasn't on my list of things to do, especially after the terrible night of sleep I had. It was a family business, though, and those of us who didn't work full time here still tried to help out when we could.

My dad was getting older and couldn't do what he used to, so it was even more imperative we all pitched in. Brody lived in California now, so he wasn't around. Bear just got back from college where he got his business degree, so his time was limited, and Brock was the manager here at the shop and practically lived in his office. As for Baker....well, he was supposed to be finishing up getting his mechanic's license, but he was too busy fuckin' around to be reliable. I got it; we all did. Baker had been through some shit over the past ten years. Him being the youngest and getting the least amount of time with our mom had really messed him up. And him feeling responsible because she was driving home early because she caught the flu that he had didn't help anything either. We were all just hoping that he would grow out of the immaturity, but he was showing no signs yet.

My recently turned twenty-one-year-old brother shook his head and grabbed his keys. "You're becoming such an old man, Beau."

"Fuck you, Baker. I'm tired. I worked all week, and now I'm here helping y'all get caught up." And I slept like shit because I dreamed about Georgia all night, but there was no way in hell I was telling him that.

"I work."

I laughed and slid back under the car. "Speaking of you not working, talked to Grayson yesterday."

He grunted. "It wasn't a big deal."

"Really? So you going to Lawless and getting wasted and starting a fight isn't a big deal?"

"No, it's not. And that's not what happened anyway. I was merely lookin' to score but apparently tried talkin' to the wrong woman. Her man got up in my face, and if Grayson hadn't been there, I'd have kicked his ass. Then gone home with his girl." He snickered, and I shook my head in disappointment even though he couldn't see me.

"How about if you're lookin' to score, you stay local so

if you get wasted, I can come and get you instead of you crashing on Gray's couch for the night and ruining one of the few nights he's off duty?" I yanked on my wrench, but my hands were too damn oily, and it slipped. "Shit."

"I had to go there, Beau. I need to diversify my portfolio."

I wiped my hands on my pants. "You mean the women here have all talked and deemed you a pig so nobody will sleep with you."

"Um, no. That's not what's happened at all. I think it's the other way around, and my big brother is jealous he's lost his game?" His booted foot kicked my own.

The truth was, he couldn't be more wrong. I was so sick of the bar scene. The same shit every time. Spend money buying drinks for a woman to find out she either never had intentions of coming home with me or she gets so drunk she can't even walk by the end of the night... And I'm not into fucking women who can't tell me how good my cock feels. But then when a woman actually holds her liquor and comes home with me, she never wants to leave. It's a no-win situation.

There was only one woman I'd ever wanted, but the history was so ugly I didn't think I could ever look past it to get down to the beauty of what we used to have together.

"Not jealous, Baker. Just sick of it."

He snorted. "Sure, you are."

"Don't try to change the subject. I'm actually kind of worried about your dumb ass."

"I'm all good, bro. You can chill." He flashed a grin. "You can also come on down to The Tap tonight."

I really didn't want to. "I'm damn tired, Baker."

"So like I said, you've lost your game."

"I have not."

His laughter echoed in the garage, and I gritted my teeth, knowing what was about to come out of his mouth.

"Care to make a friendly bet? That is, unless you're too scared." His knuckles cracked, and we'd done this enough times that I knew he was standing with his arms crossed and an eyebrow raised.

And since us Bradford brothers could never back down from a bet, I placed my wager. Plus, I'd be able to keep an eye on him. Despite what he said, I thought something was going on with him. "Fine, shit stain. I'll meet you in an hour. First one to score." Finding someone to get my mind off Georgia wasn't a bad idea, actually.

"Deal," he agreed. "But I get to decide who you pick up first."

"No way. I don't trust you enough."

"You should 'cause if I pick someone good for you, you could easily screw me over and pick a dog for me."

Whatever. "Fine."

"Great. See you soon." He whistled as he walked out, and as much as I hated that *this* was why he was happy, I was just glad he was. He'd been different ever since Georgia left, and over the years, he'd gone from one extreme to the next, and I was really hoping that he'd learn before he made a mistake he couldn't just walk away from.

The Tap was the only bar in our small town of Warrenville, but the tourists staying at the cabins on the outskirts frequented it. Folks from Lawless also came here a lot, and as they started building subdivisions on the other side of town, we'd seen an uptick in not only customers but petty crime as well. And I didn't like that at all. None of the locals did.

I pulled into the dirt parking lot and stepped out of my truck. It was the same one I had ten years ago, but now it was totally restored. Everything except the bench seat because I had good memories on there, and I refused to change that.

When I opened the heavy cherry wood door, every head turned, and when the locals recognized me, a multitude of waves and hellos filtered through the old rickety building. I nodded back, giving a wink to a couple of women who always make it a point to get my attention. I only had to venture halfway through the bar before I found a few of my brothers, each with a tight dress already glued to their arm.

"I see you got a head start on our bet." I raised my chin at Baker.

"Nope."

He poured me a beer from the pitcher, and I drank half of it in a few swallows. I shook hands with my other brothers, Bear and Brock, who both had guilty smirks on their faces.

"What?"

"Nothing, man. I'm just happy to see ya." Baker was the first to speak up.

"I saw you an hour ago. What's going on?" I looked at Brock, the middle kid, but he pretended to tie his shoe.

"Bear."

"Yeah?" he asked.

"The fuck's goin' on?"

The moment the words left my mouth, a flash of light blinded me when the door opened, and a hush filled the bar. I blinked the stars away to see what everyone was focused on and almost dropped my beer.

"Fuck me," I muttered under my breath.

"Precisely." Baker concurred. "You must get *her* to fuck *you*."

Georgia Westbury had made her presence known. The vixen showed up after ten years and walked into this bar like she fuckin' owned the place. Everyone hugged and welcomed her back, but nobody knew what she did to me. To my family. How she just up and left without even talking to me. Seeing her last night didn't change the way I felt about her. If anything, it reminded me why I held such disdain for the woman.

My brothers laughed, but I shook my head. "No way, Baker. I'm not touchin' her."

"A bet's a bet, Beau. No backing out now," he reminded me with a shrug.

She must have heard him, maybe she even recognized his voice even though it had gotten deeper over the years, and glanced our way. The easy smile she was

141

wearing dissolved instantly when she spotted me, and it sucked more than I thought it would from me knowing I was the reason she wasn't happy anymore.

And then I remembered why I was even here in the first place.

I set my beer down and took a threatening step toward Baker. It didn't matter that I was a cop, but I was his big brother, and I could still whoop his punk ass if it came down to it. He set the chick aside and rose to his full height to meet me, nose to nose. "What the hell do you think you're doin'?"

An evil yet sympathetic smirk formed on his lips, and as much as I wanted to slap that look off his face, I couldn't. Not in public anyway. It wouldn't look too good for an officer of the law to get into a bar brawl. "Pretend all you want, but you haven't moved on, and you haven't been the same since she left. You need to deal with *your* shit, brother."

"This is low, *especially for* you." He was the one who was destroyed when she left, almost more than I was.

"You don't seem surprised to see her," Baker remarked.

"Because I'm not. I knew she was back."

He rocked back on his heels. "She looks good, doesn't she? All filled out, her tits are nice and tight... Probably hasn't had kids yet, which means her pu—"

"Shut your fuckin' mouth, Baker."

"Ah, you don't give a shit about her, so why do you care if I express my appreciation?"

I shook my head. "You were raised better than to talk like that about any woman."

"Oh, okay. So it's not about you caring, it's about me being disrespectful. I see. Would it be okay if I go over there and sweet-talk her fine ass into my bed tonight as long as I say please and open the door for her?"

"You really want your brother's seconds, be my guest," I spat.

He crossed his arms. "Thought you were raised better than to talk like that about a woman."

"Baker, that's enough." Bear tried to shut him up.

"Okay, you're right. I'll stop talking now." He peered around me, and I knew when he lifted his chin, he was doing it at her. "Be right back, or maybe I won't."

I grabbed his arm and yanked him the couple of inches until his shoulder slammed against mine. "I'm done. You put yourself in the position you can't drive, I swear on Mom's grave if you get behind the wheel of your car, I'll send that mofo off to salvage and buy you a bus pass with the money I get for it."

Ignoring the calls from Bear, I skirted around Baker and headed toward the side entrance.

For him to say I hadn't moved on was jacked. I'd totally moved on from her and her wrath. That was ridiculous. Just like her. Ridiculously sexy and ridiculously beautiful. I'd never in my life been as affected by a woman as I had her. I was so pissed at myself that she was back only twenty-four hours, and I felt the same as I did the day I found out she left town.

Damn, though. He was right. I'd never been able to let it go, and as much as I missed her and wanted her back, I just couldn't get over what she did to me and how easily she disposed of me. It made me feel like the trash she used to tell me I was.

"Beau."

I stopped in my tracks and turned to see her running toward me like a chick in a romance movie. Her blond hair blowing in the wind and dust kicking beneath her feet.

"This isn't the definition of a wide berth, Gigi."

She skidded to a stop a few feet in front of me and swayed a bit, practically panting. "I haven't stopped thinking about you."

"Bullshit."

"It's true."

I pinched the bridge of my nose and gave myself a breath before I said something I was going to regret. "You sure know how to show it, huh?" I didn't try to hide the sarcasm.

"Since the day I left, I thought about you constantly. I missed you, I wished you would have come to me, and I... and I wanted to say this yesterday, but I totally chickened out. You know how I need to talk myself up before I have conversations with people—"

"That's not true 'cause it turns out I don't know you as well as I thought I did."

She sucked in a breath and ran her hands through her hair without acknowledging what I had just said. "I know I promised I'd give you a wide berth, but I have to tell you… You *deserve* to know."

This wasn't her simply trying to make herself feel better for what she did. Something was not right, and I couldn't deny the primal need I had to protect her, and took a step closer when I noticed the raw pain etched on her beautiful face.

She backed up and held her hands out. "No. You… I… you need to know. I didn't leave because I wanted to. I had to. Because he … he threatened you, too, and…"

Reaching out, I grabbed her arms, focusing deep into her eyes and seeing all-consuming panic. "Georgia, calm down."

"You need to know. It's safe to tell you now." Of course it was safe. Her father was dead.

"Stop," I growled. Scanning to make sure nobody was around to gossip about us being together, and because she looked like she was about to have a meltdown, I led her to my truck. "We'll talk at my house." I opened the passenger door. "Get in."

She shook her head. "We can do this here. I swear I'll be fast."

"No, we can't. Get in. I'll take you wherever you want to go after, but right now, I need you to get in so we can get out of here before someone comes out and hears us." The things we needed to talk about were private. Nobody needed to know our secrets.

"Fine." She steeled her spine. "I took a cab here anyway…"

ANNA BROOKS

I closed the door behind her and rushed around to my side. "Is this the same truck? It looks like it, but it's like... new or something."

"Same truck." I glanced at the bracelet that she gave me by braiding the leather strands from an old baseball glove of mine together. It was looped onto my gearshift and hadn't moved for over a decade.

"So cool." She whispered the words to herself, and I didn't give her more than that. I hated that I loved her being next to me, but I'd have been a damn liar if I told myself it wasn't good to have her so close again. I broke a few traffic laws getting to my place, and when I rolled down my driveway, she sat up and gaped at the six acres my home was on. "Wow. This is yours?"

"Yeah." I pulled into my garage and shut my baby off. "Bought the land about five years ago and just finished building last summer. Took a while but I'm happy with it."

She followed me in from the garage to the attached mudroom where she kicked off her shoes. "You can keep them on."

"No, I don't want to dirty these beautiful floors. What are they?"

I paused, tossing my keys on the kitchen counter around the corner. "It's just tile, Georgia."

"But they look like wood. Wow."

"But they're not, so you can walk on them with shoes."

She shook her head. "I'm fine."

"You want a beer?"

"Why not? Might make this easier."

I grabbed two bottles from the fridge and motioned for her to follow me, refusing to acknowledge how great it was having her here. In the house I built imagining a family I made with her living in it. She studied my relatively bare house with appreciation and actually turned in a circle when we reached the living room. "Oh my God."

I handed her a beer and sat in my favorite leather chair, resting my ankle on my knee. "I know. It's big."

She rolled her eyes at my playful tone, and I chastised myself for letting my guard down already. "Boys and their toys. How big is it?"

My brow shot up, and I bit my lip.

"Oh, stop." She slashed her hand through the air. "I already know *that*." And Christ if my dick didn't twitch. "I'm talking about the TV. It takes up the entire wall."

"Eighty-five inches." I leaned back and took a swallow while she did the same, but she was rocking back and forth nervously. As soon as she gave me her attention again, I sat up and sighed. "I know, Georgia."

Her expression was almost unreadable, but the tightness in her body gave away the fear she was trying to conceal.

"I've known since you left."

"But—"

How could she think I could just let her go without knowing why? "Christ, we made plans to spend the rest of our lives together, and you never showed up. I lost my damn mind with worry when you didn't come to my house that night, so I went to yours, and your mom

147

answered the door. She told me that you left because your dad found out about us and went crazy with threats toward you and me and my family. And because he was friends with Judge Clancy, you decided his threats had merit and left."

She abruptly pivoted and walked over to the sliding glass door that led out to my oversized back patio. There was a small pond in the backyard, but otherwise, nothing but green grass and lots of trees in the distance. "If you know that, why do you still hate me, then?"

"I don't hate you. I could *never* hate you. It was clearly what you wanted and who was I to try to change your mind? You'd lived with a monster for your entire life and it was your chance to get free, so the last thing I wanted to do was hold you back from that. But fuck, Gigi, you abandoned me. Us… Baker. We had plans, a future, and you threw it all away without even coming to say goodbye!"

Her shoulders shaking with emotion, she choked out, "I didn't have a choice. He was going to hurt you."

"I know you think that, but you didn't even give me a chance to decide whether I wanted to go with you or not."

She spun around and raised a brow. "Would you have?"

When I didn't answer, she pressed her lips together as if to prove her point.

"I had responsibilities here, a family, siblings to take care of. I couldn't just leave, and you know that. But for you, I would have."

She swallowed. "I could never ask you to do that."

"You never gave me the choice," I gritted out.

"Then what difference would it have made?"

"It could have made all the difference in the world, Georgia." The pain of feeling abandoned by her came through in my gruff tone.

She looked at the ceiling. "Do you think I *wanted* to leave?"

"I think you thought I'd follow you because of how much I fuckin' loved you."

Her neck flushed. "I didn't think you'd follow me, but I did think you'd at least come and find me once in the past ten years."

I waited a beat before I responded because if I didn't, I was going to say something I'd regret. "And I'd have thought you would have come and at least said goodbye before you left."

"And what would that have done, Beau? Huh?" She stormed over to me and stood at my feet, cheeks pink, heaving angry breaths. "Would me coming to tell you the same thing my mom did have changed anything?"

I stood, our chests brushing on my way up, and cocked my head to the side. "We'll never know, will we?"

"I guess not." She sighed in dismay and shocked the shit out of me when her forehead landed on my chest.

It took all of my strength, and some I didn't know I had, not to pull her closer. Or tip her face up and slam my mouth to hers. I kept my hands fisted at my side and let her get out what she needed to so this could maybe be over once and for all.

149

"Would you really have come with me? If I came to you and said that Tad threat—"

"*Tad*?" I grabbed her arms and pushed her back so I could see her face. She tilted her head up and startled, frightened eyes found mine. "What the fuck does Tad have anything to do with this?"

CHAPTER 12

Georgia

"**D**ID HE THREATEN YOU?"

Shit. I knew I needed to tell him the truth, but sensing the ire vibrating from his body made me question if it was the right thing to do. I should have just let him think it was my father like he had all these years.

"Gigi, what the fuck does Tad have to do with it?"

I jumped at the harsh edge of his voice and remembered why I didn't tell him in the first place. Beau had an explosive temper, and for such a reserved guy, it was shocking to see the first time back in high school when those guys were picking on his brother.

When he stopped Tad from raping me, he was a different kind of mad. It was controlled, and somehow, even after what I'd just gone through, I felt so safe with him.

But when he found out that my dad hit me, that was something else. He scared me because the rage rolling off him was raw and unbridled and wildly unpredictable. I wasn't scared of him but scared *for* him, that he'd do something he'd regret.

"Tell me!" Even him yelling at me, I knew down to my bones that he would never hurt me. I reached behind me and found a footstool, then lowered myself onto it. My legs were like rubber.

I lifted my head and swallowed, barely unable to form a word with how dry my throat was. "Tad found out about us and threatened to tell my dad."

"Why would you care if Tad told him? You were going to anyway."

"I was."

He pinched the bridge of his nose. "So again, why the hell would you care if Tad told your dad?"

"I didn't."

"You're not making sense, Gigi."

I wasn't sure if telling him the truth would make things worse, but he deserved to know. "I was there that night, when you came to the house and my mom told you, you know?"

He blinked. "What?" Then his jaw dropped.

"She told you I had just left, but I didn't. I was there, standing behind the door, crying, listening to her tell you that my dad found out and how he went crazy."

I remembered that like it was yesterday, I dreamed about it constantly. *"Not only did he threaten Georgia, he also threatened your family, your dad, you… and we decided it was best for everyone, but especially her, if she went away for a little while."* That was what my mom told him. That was the lie. And God… the way Beau's voice cracked when he listened to her say that I left. The disbelief that I caved to my dad's threats. The sadness when he finally accepted that I'd made up my mind and was already gone. It nearly destroyed me. *"I don't care about me, but if he's going to just keep hurting her, and she's so afraid she had to leave without even saying goodbye, then I guess I have no choice but to let her go."* I had heard him sniffle, and my mom said his eyes were wet, but after he said that, he walked to his truck with his head down and drove away.

That was the hardest thing I ever had to do; stand there, listening to my mom lying to scare the love of my life away from me. It was more painful than getting knocked out by Tad hours earlier. But it had to be done.

Beau tilted his head and scrutinized my every breath for what seemed like hours. I used to love that, how he was able to simply know what I was feeling with just a glance. Nobody in my entire life was ever able to depict my feelings or fears without me having to tell them.

But now, trying to keep something from him, I was kind of wishing over the years he had lost some of his sense of awareness when it came to me. "You're lying."

"Beau…"

He squatted down in front of me, and it was like an understanding hit him that I never wanted any of this. I didn't want to leave, and I always wanted him. "You're lying. *Your mom lied.* Christ, how the fuck did I never see that?"

Silence loomed heavy, and I closed my eyes, unable

153

to face him even though I had dreamed of having him this close again for the past ten years.

"Look at me, Georgia." His voice was soft. "Gigi, look at me."

"No."

"There's more, isn't there? You didn't just disappear because of your father. No... something else happened that made you leave after I dropped you off that day. What was it?" God, he was going to figure this part out. "It was something else. Or someone else. It was Tad."

My breath hitched, and he growled, the vibration traveling from his throat and down his arms, all the way to the palms of his hands resting on my thighs. "You said he threatened to tell your dad, but that's not it, either. What did he do to you?"

I couldn't bring myself to answer. I'd forced it away for so long that I almost forgot it was there. Even though the scar was on my face when I saw my reflection in the mirror, even though I never got the image out of my head, even though every morning when I woke up in a bed that wasn't Beau's, I remembered.

"What the fuck did he do to you?"

"*He attacked me!*" I jumped up and screamed the admission, dropping my bottle of beer to the floor, glass shattering and amber liquid raining. "And he made damn sure there was no way I could cover the bruises up. He knew if you saw me, you'd go after him. He wanted you to hurt him because he knew he could get you out of the picture so he could have me."

Beau's head wobbled. "What do you mean *have* you?"

"My dad owed Judge Clancy, and his payback was an arranged marriage between Tad and me for reasons I don't even care to know."

"You've gotta be joking." He rolled the words down his tongue slowly.

"I'm not. And even if I stayed and did the unthinkable and broke up with you, there was no way I could live in the same town and not be with you. I was terrified that I would end up just like my mother, and I did not want her miserable life. I was terrified of what he would do to me if you were behind bars. And I was terrified of what *you* would do to him." I covered my face with my hands and sobbed, "I was terrified of everything, Beau, and I didn't know what to do. My mom offered me the out, and I took it because I was so fucking scared of what would happen if I stayed."

It was so quiet that I couldn't even hear Beau breathing, but I knew he was here because his fingers were digging into my skin. "Look at me."

I finally lifted my head and wasn't surprised to find every molecule of his face tight and flushed in anger. He cupped my jaw and ran his thumb softly across the small scar on my cheekbone. "Tad is why you left?"

"Yes."

"He *hurt* you."

He wasn't asking, but I had to tell him what he already knew. "Yes." I sniffled. "As soon as you pulled away from my house… he must have been following me or something. I loved you too much to take the chance that you would do exactly what he wanted. I knew you would. I knew you wouldn't let him get away with it, no matter what the consequences to you were." I gave him an imploring look, desperate for him to understand. "Don't you see, Beau? I couldn't be the reason you went to jail. I'd rather you have had a broken heart than one that wasn't beating because, for all I knew, that was a possibility if Tad got his way."

"I wish you'd have told me."

Pressing my lips together, I shook my head. "It wouldn't have mattered. If I stayed, you would have taken one look at me and lost your mind, and no matter how much I would have begged you not to, you'd still go after Tad."

"You're right. I would have. And in a fucked-up way, I understand why you did what you did, but you and your mom still should have told me. I deserved to know."

"I never understood her until she told me about how she and your dad couldn't be together back then—" I cut myself off because I didn't know if he knew. Even in the thick of all the emotion surrounding us, he chuckled.

"I know. Dad told me after you left. Confessed it all to me and helped me to understand better. Kinda crazy, isn't it? Our parents young and in love and forbidden from being together."

It was sad, really. "It is, but it also made me understand things so much more. Their situation was the same, but it wasn't. My options—"

"What about mine?" he reminded me. "I wasn't given a choice about anything. I didn't even have the full story to make any kind of decision."

I pressed my lips together and nodded, "I know."

"Does your father have anything at all to do with why you left?"

"Nope. Believe it or not, he never found out about us, at least not that I know of. He walked into years of pent-up anger and hostility from my mom after she found me beaten up, and she went all psycho on him."

He flinched angrily. "If you were supposed to marry Tad, why'd your dad let you go so easily?"

"Money. Mom gave him an ultimatum. Either let me go and she'd use the money from a trust he didn't know about to pay off his debt with the agreement Tad leaves me alone, or force me to marry him and she'd empty her accounts out."

He grinned. "Sorry, but that's kind of badass."

"I know. I'd never seen her so upset. And naturally, since my father was such a selfish bastard, he picked the money, thank God. The marriage thing was for business, which I guess wasn't as important as his debt. We honestly never talked about it again. I think I was hoping if I didn't, it would just go away, and it did."

"Thank God for that."

"Mom had secretly kept me enrolled in college and got me set up to start that fall. I graduated, got a nursing job, and lived a boring, lonely life. But I missed you every day. I picked up the phone a million times to call you…and I slept with the one picture I had of us together. Then when my mom told me Tad had gotten arrested, I knew it was safe to return. It had been eating me alive that you didn't know the truth all these years, and now that he's behind bars, you can't do something stupid to him."

"Your dad dying had nothing to do with you coming back?"

My throat was dry despite the acid swirling in my stomach and splashing up into my esophagus as I relived all of the shit from my past. "No. I hadn't seen him since that night. It was just coincidence that he died the same week Tad was arrested."

Time froze and apprehension gnawed away at any hope I still held tight. His body was locked tight, including any indication of what he was feeling. I used to think I knew him, but I had no idea what was going on in his mind right then.

"You're right," he finally whispered. "I would have killed him. I swear, if you'd have come to me all bruised and bloody because of him, I'd have lost it. It would have been the only thing I could do because beyond physically hurting him, there wasn't anything else I would have been capable of back then. But that was ten years ago. Things have changed."

"What do you mean?"

Leading me to the couch, he sat us down. "Why do you think I became a cop?"

"I don't know."

I almost forgot what his touch did to me, but when he tucked some hair behind my ear and cupped my jaw, the flutter in my belly took my breath away. "I told you I'd get to him one day, and I did."

Oh God. "What did you do?"

He ran his tongue across his teeth, and something intriguing shifted in his eyes. "What I had to." And then before I could blink, his mouth was on mine again.

Finally.

I gasped on a shocked but deliciously surprised moan, and his tongue found its way to dance with my own. In the midst of it all, I was pushed back onto the couch. My fingers dove into his hair, and I held him close, desperate for him not to leave me. Clawing at him to make sure he was real and this wasn't a dream. His hands explored me straight up my sides, his thumbs brushing over my taut nipples until they reached my jaw, where he cupped my face.

His hard body pressed into mine, and I arched into him, yearning for every part of him I could get. For every moment to last forever.

He slid a hand down between my breasts, then over them, cupping one tight, grunting at its weight in his hand. Next, he moved to the other, and instead of him verbally expressing his approval, he pressed himself against me, showing me with his hard crotch rubbing exactly where I needed him to be that he was as turned on as I was.

"God." I tore my mouth from his to suck in air but

quickly realized I wasn't light-headed because I wasn't getting enough oxygen. It was because I was with him again, and just the thought of it made me breathless.

"More." He squeezed my jaw and yanked my mouth back over so he could cover it and slid his tongue inside again.

A rush of wetness made my thighs quiver, and I was flying through the air but sinking at the same time. One hand to my ass and the other to the back of my head, keeping my lips to his as he practically ran to his bedroom with me in his arms, where he tossed me onto the bed.

"Get naked. I'd do it, but I don't want to waste the time."

Neither did I. Whipping my shirt off, I watched as he did the same. His hungry gaze flew to my bra, and when I released the clasp on the back and it fell down my arms, his muscular abdominals flexed, and it was impossible not to notice the sheen of sweat pebbling on his chest.

We both undid the clasps on our belts and slid our zippers down. Then he shoved his pants and boxers to his thighs, and I got distracted from what I was supposed to be doing when his long, hard cock sprung free and slapped against his toned stomach. The next thing I knew, he was tugging at the ankles of my jeans and ripped them off.

"Spread your legs, Gigi."

"Beau." I was suddenly nervous, but not unsure if I

wanted him. It was just... it had been so long. Ten years to be exact. After him, there was no one. Not because I was waiting for him or anything, but I never found someone I wanted to share my body with more than a kiss. I didn't trust anybody, and I just didn't want anyone else.

My heart was always with him, and another man simply never appealed to me.

"Georgia, spread."

I bit my lip and slowly opened my legs. As they were barely apart, he grabbed my hips, pulled me up, and closed his mouth over my panties. "Oh my God." My breath swooshed out of my lungs as the pressure from my core pulsed throughout my entire body, igniting a fire that had been simmering for a decade.

"Sorry, babe." I shifted my head down just in time to see him tear my thong in half. His eyes on mine, he lowered his head just enough and ran his tongue between my folds, and I knew if he kept his mouth on me for one more second, I would have come from just that. But he pulled his neck back and crawled over me, kicking his jeans off all the way. "Can't wait." The fact that he couldn't drop his pants before he tasted me made my belly tighten, desperate for him to be inside me, squeezing him and never letting him go again.

He dropped his forehead against mine, one arm straight out next to my head, holding himself up, and grabbed his cock with the other. "You good?" he asked through gritted teeth.

"More than." I pushed up. "Please."

The head of his dick prodded against my quivering opening, and a long moan whispered through my parted lips.

"Christ." He pushed in just enough for me to feel the tip. "So goddamn perfect, Georgia."

I was prepared, but I wasn't, and when he pulsed his hips, hard, I screamed in pleasured pain as he slammed himself inside me. All the way. *Finally.* I fantasized about it and missed him being inside me for so long that I almost forgot what it felt like.

"Did I hurt you?"

I snapped back to a reality I never thought I'd be in again, and the look on his face—the raw, primal need—made any tinge of pain I had go away, knowing I did that to him. My heart nearly burst at the knowledge that this big, strong, powerful man could be pushed to his limit, but still took the time to care about me.

I wound my legs around him, and he managed to slide in even deeper. "It's been a while, but you could never hurt me."

He ground his pelvis, and hissed, "How long?"

"Ten years."

His entire body stopped vibrating, and he completely froze. A drop of sweat fell onto my chest from his forehead, burning desire in its wake. Eyes blazing bright, he whispered, "No."

"Yes, Beau." I met his eyes, blinking back tears. "I never wanted anyone else."

"Baby." He collapsed on top of me and wrapped his arms tight across my back, then rolled us over. His soft touch glided down my sides until he clamped my hips and sat me up. Then one hand came up and he held my face, the other slid around and zeroed in on my clit.

I fell forward, my palms on his chest and felt it building already. "Beau." I panted, my hips rocking on their own accord. God, him inside me, filling me, *completing* me, was the best feeling in the entire world.

"There you go." He circled harder, deeper, and moaned louder, rocked faster. "Take that."

And when it hit me, I couldn't even hold myself up. I collapsed forward as everything inside me exploded, the pleasure so overwhelming it literally stole the air from my lungs.

"Yeah, baby," he encouraged. "Ride that out but get ready 'cause I'm not done yet."

That made another current score through me, sharp and hot.

He held my hips in his hands and slammed up into me. "Shit." I tried to push up, but he clamped one arm around me like a vise.

"Stay still, Gigi. Let me fuck you." He crashed into me again and again, and my thighs spasmed as my pussy clenched. "Fuck, yeah." I wrapped my arms around him, and he growled, low and guttural as his hips pistoned fast and so, so deep. Every time he bottomed out, I felt it building again.

The climax was going to be explosive, and I knew it

would destroy me, ruin me more than the last one did. There would be no coming back from this, from him, from what he did to me. Not that there ever was, but it was even worse now. Because this was... this was something I didn't even know existed.

"I've got you, Gigi. Just relax, baby. Let it happen." He tightened his grip on my hip, all the while not letting up on his rhythm. Pounding into me from below, he rubbed against my clit, and the delicious friction made my toes tingle. "Who's got you?"

"You do."

"*Who?*"

"You."

He groaned and pumped into me so hard that if he wasn't holding me, I'd have flown out of the damn window. "Say my name, Georgia. Tell me who's fucking you. Tell me who's got you. Tell me who won't let you go again."

"You, Beau. It's always been you."

He growled and shoved his face in my neck, hitting the exact right spot over and over, and we came together, spiraling, crashing, falling over the edge; two bodies molded into one, hearts pounding against one another and souls reconnecting even though the reality is they were never far apart. His grip was relentless as he shuddered, and I hoped he left a mark so when I woke up in the morning and saw it, I'd know it wasn't a dream.

"I missed you," I whispered. "I missed you so damn much."

He rolled us over, still connected, and pushed the hair off my face. The love shining at me was more than I ever hoped and better than I could have imagined. "I was lost without you, Gigi. Everything I did was for you, and I always thought that if I made this town safe, you'd come back. We missed out on a lot of time, but I promise I'll make it up to you... until the day I die."

CHAPTER 13

Beau

GEORGIA'S WEIGHT IN MY ARMS FELT PERFECT. IT always did. And as much as I didn't want to leave her right now, I had to. Too much fury flowed through me to stay still. All night, I'd stared at the ceiling, unable to get a wink of sleep.

The thought of that piece of shit being the reason she left and why we lost out on so much time with each other made me uncontrollably livid. My hands were tied ten years ago, but they weren't anymore. So I was going to use them for exactly what I told her I would.

As careful as I could, I slid my arm out from beneath her and slyly rolled out of bed. I put a pillow at her back to hopefully give her some comfort so she didn't wake up, and then grabbed my clothes. Shutting the door behind me, I got dressed in the hallway.

What I needed to do wouldn't take long, and she was never a morning person, so I was just praying she still slept late and didn't wake up while I was gone.

After arming my security system, I got in my truck and headed toward Lawless, the sun rising as I drove. Luckily, where I needed to get to was close to the end of the county line, but I still got there faster than I should have. When I pulled up to the prison, I took a quick look around and was relieved to see Grayson was walking out. I should have been at work, too, but I took a few vacation days after the night I had.

"What the hell are you doing here?" He stopped at the bottom of the steps.

"I need to see him."

He leaned back and crossed his arms. "By the sound of your voice, I'd say that's probably the last thing you need."

"It's *exactly* what I need."

He didn't budge, and after a stare down, I muttered, "Georgia's back."

"Shit, seriously?"

"Yup. And she told me why she left. The *real* reason."

He tilted his head and expelled a breath when he connected the dots. "Tad." In order to have Grayson and his buds keep an eye out for the douchebag, I had to tell him everything that happened with Georgia. And I knew he'd have my back because we were friends.

"He hurt her, man. Knocked her out. She left because she was afraid of him, what I'd do to him if I found out, and has been livin' in fear for a decade." I paused and took a breath. "Let me in there."

"No."

I leaned forward, tightening my fists so hard my knuckles turned white. "I need to do this."

He studied me a minute, glanced at his watch, then scrubbed his hands down his face. "I can't even guarantee I can get you back there, but I'll try. If I do, this isn't carte blanche. You can't break anything, and you gotta be quick."

Lifting my chin, I stood to my full height and waited for him to lead the way. We walked through the prison and I showed my badge, and Grayson stopped and talked to a guard, who handed him an ID badge. I waited about five minutes for the shift change, and then we snuck in.

Since Tad's daddy was just as big of a douchebag as him, he tried but couldn't get him out of the charges. He did manage to get his son a cell away from gen pop, complete with a television, though.

Tad might have the pleasure of watching a screen all day, but I had the pleasure of watching his face blanch in terror when Grayson slid opened the door to his cell without a word, and I stepped in.

My back was to the kitchen, but I heard her feet pitter-pattering toward me. "Morning." She slid her dainty hands around to my chest, resting her head on the middle of my back, and I felt the weight of the world roll off my shoulders with that simple touch.

I shut the burner off and turned around, not wanting to miss a second of seeing her beautiful face. "Mornin',

Gigi." She tilted her head back and offered her mouth, which I gladly took. Her lips seared a path of liquid fire down my spine, settling in my dick with the desire to pump it into her any way I could.

She pulled away, breathless, and ran her tongue across her lips. "You should have woken me when you got up."

Little did she know I'd been up for hours already. "You needed the sleep."

I brushed some of her hair off her shoulder, but she grabbed my wrist. "What happened to your hand?" *Shit.*

"Nothing."

I tried to pull it away, but she yanked it back. "Your knuckles are all scraped up. What happened?"

"I said nothing. Just drop it." This time, I actually put some strength into it and separated my arm from her grip.

Her suspicious gaze turned angry, and she marched over to the dining room that was never used and whipped open the curtains. I hated to admit that even though she was furious, I couldn't help but stare at her luscious behind in her tight jeans. "Your truck isn't in the same place it was last night. Did you go out to get food this morning?"

"No."

She pursed her lips. "Leave to get me a toothbrush?"

"I have a bunch of extras for when one of my brothers crashes here."

She looked over her shoulder, and I lifted my eyes so quickly she didn't see me checking out her ass when she was in this state. "Please tell me you didn't do what I think you did."

"Depends. What do you think I did?"

"Did you go beat him up?"

I crossed my arms, and she turned and leaned on the window, glaring at me as she awaited my answer, but already knowing it. "Not exactly."

"Beau." Her fists slammed down at her sides, and her cheeks flushed. "Why did you do that? God, you weren't supposed to do that. Now you're going to get—"

"I'm not gonna get anything, Gigi."

Something about how she stared at me in disappointment wasn't right. She wasn't mad. She was... worried. Anxious. And she was supposed to live easy with me. Things should have been simple and smooth, and I was failing at that already. "I'm going home." She punched at her cell phone screen a few times, then stormed past the kitchen to get her shoes, shoved her feet in them, and then flipped her hair at me as she opened the front door.

"What the fuck?" I muttered to myself. My head spun at the turn of events, but I got my ass in gear real quick and chased after her. "Georgia!"

She twirled and almost fell down the porch steps. "That's why I didn't tell you. Exactly why. I didn't want you to go after him. You don't know what he's capable of—"

"Yeah, babe... actually, I do. Why do you think it took this long for his rat ass to get locked up?"

"Let's talk about that." She pointed at me. "Tell me all about how he ended up there in the first place."

I raised a brow at the sass but leaned a shoulder on the doorjamb and answered her. "I watched him. His patterns and routines. It didn't take me long to realize he drove drunk a lot. I pulled him over for that a few times. Each time, he failed the breathalyzer, and I cuffed him and threw him in the back of my vehicle and brought him in. And each time, he was released within hours scot-free with no repercussions because of his daddy.

"He started going to Lawless 'cause I was on his ass so much, but I have a friend. And that friend has friends. None of us like the piece of shit spoiled rich daddy's boys who get away with breaking the law and assaulting women. So needless to say, when they got him for a DUI there, when he was arrested, he couldn't get out. And the judge was none too happy that he'd been released three other times, so his sentence wasn't lenient and he's now doing his time at the prison in Lawless. *That's* how it happened."

"But you didn't know what he did to me," she stated.

"Georgia, he almost raped you, and then he had me arrested. What else did I need to know? I told you I'd find a way to make him pay."

A sigh whispered through her lips. "How did you get to him today?"

"Like I said, I have a friend. He has access, there was a shift change, and I got in and out fast. That's it."

Her shoulders fell forward. "I need to go home."

"Why?"

"I think it'd be best for us to have some time apart right now. Things are so new, and I just… I feel like maybe telling you was a mistake because this is the exact opposite of what I wanted to happen."

I hauled ass out of my house and grabbed her shoulders, lifting her up the step and then dipping my head so she could see me. "It wasn't a mistake."

"Beau, I don't want him to have anything on you. And the last thing I need is to have to constantly worry that he's going to get out and retaliate again. Because you and I both know he won't be locked up forever, and when he gets out, he's going to be even madder than he was before." She was starting to panic, and I wasn't liking the change in attitude. She'd been sweet and reflective before, but this sudden onset of regret was not cool. "Maybe I should just go. It's not smart or safe for me to be here after all. I came back to finally tell you the truth and be with you, not have him come between us again."

I lifted a hand and took hold of the back of her head so she couldn't avoid me, ignoring what she said about going back because she was *not* leaving. "You came back to be with me?"

Like I knew she would, she tried to pull away.

"Answer me. That's why you came back? Because you wanted to be with me." I thought it was because she was here to help her mom, but secretly hoping it was because of me.

Tears pooled in her eyes, and she nodded. "It's only ever been you."

Something struck me at the moment, and I realized I never asked her. "Why did you wait so long?"

"What?"

"You talked to your mom, so you had to have known I was a cop. You knew I would have been able to protect you from him, but you waited. For years, you waited to come to me. No calls. Not a letter or postcard. You never even sent an email."

"Let me go."

I released my grip and took a step back. "Why?"

"It doesn't matter."

I dug in my heels. "Why, Georgia?"

"Because I was scared you were going to reject me, just like you did!" she cried. "I knew how upset you were, and I was afraid you wouldn't understand or for-give me. I figured you'd throw it in my face, and if you did that, I couldn't survive it. And if I saw you with an-other woman? God, I couldn't… I waited for you for so long, all I wanted was you. *Ever.* I thought what we had was something special—"

"It was."

She combed her fingers through her hair. "From the number of women parading in and out of your house, it proves what you said to be true."

"I was mad when I said that. Jesus, look around you. This isn't a bachelor pad, it's a home for a family." I held my arms out. "You're the only woman who's ever been here, so I don't know where you're getting your informa-tion from, and it took me less than twenty-four hours to give in to you. If you think I wasn't waiting for you, then you're outta your damn mind."

"You weren't waiting," she huffed. "I know that much."

No fuckin' way, she was not goin' there. "You need to think long and hard about where this conversation is headed."

And she did that. I could practically see her brain smoking from how fast it was turning, and when a car pulled up in front of my house and honked the horn, she startled, but I steeled my spine.

"Who the fuck is that?"

"My ride."

"You are not gettin' in a car with some guy you don't know."

She shrugged. "I did it all the time in Chicago."

"Well, you're not there anymore. You're not alone. You're here, and you have me."

Her lips turned up in a sad smile. "Do I, though?" She turned around and walked down the stairs and didn't look at me as she reached the car.

I jumped off the steps, and just as she was shutting the door to the back passenger seat, I gripped the top. She huffed a noise of irritation, and the driver narrowed his eyes at me, and I pointed at his pimply face. "Anything happens to her, I'll hunt you down and enjoy breaking every single bone in your body, you hear me?"

The shaggy-haired driver nodded frantically. "Y-yes."

I diverted my attention back to her. "Text me when you get home, and then take whatever time you need to get your head straight. When you're ready, I'll be here, waiting for you, like I have been for ten goddamn years."

After slamming the door, I turned my back to her and walked inside, then grabbed my keys to my truck. I maintained a distance but stayed close enough that I could see her getting dropped off at her mother's house and got inside safely.

I waited until the driver came out of the gate and it closed before turning around and heading to my dad's. "Hey, Pop."

"Heya, boy," he hollered from his usual place in the living room, and I plopped down on the recliner opposite him. "What's with the long face? Your girl is back. Shouldn't you be happy?"

I regarded him with a speculative glance. "Who told you?"

"Baker."

Figured. "Remember how I mentioned to you her mother said the reason she left was because of Holt?"

His jaw tightened at the mention of Georgia's father.

"Turns out that was all a lie."

"You're kidding me."

"Nope. Wish I was."

He sat up and held his hands in the air. "Well, did she tell you why she left?"

"Oh, yeah. Tad fucking Clancy. Holt never knew because Tad got to Georgia first and beat the shit out of her, knowing if I found out, I'd go after him. Figured then I'd be incarcerated so he'd be able to marry her without me in the way. Her mom had been planning to free her when she turned eighteen, and she lied to me, then they left. To save me from doing time, Georgia took our future away from us."

Dad's mouth was opened like a guppy right now.

"I bought their story because I knew that motherfucker had gotten physical with her in the past, but you believed it without knowing her dad had put his hands on her before. Why did you not question it at all?"

He stared at me, and I knew whatever answer he was going to give me was difficult for him.

"History repeating itself?" I guessed, prompting a reminder about Mabel and him and how they were forced apart.

"Yes."

"Mabel's dad?"

He shook his head. "Remember the original shop your granddad started? The reason he moved it into town before I took over?"

Holy shit. "Yeah. There was a fire."

"That was Holt. His warning for me to leave her alone. When that didn't stop Mabel from seeing me, her dad sent his cronies. Made her watch them knock me around until I was coughing up blood." Unspoken pain I'd never noticed was alive in his eyes, and I held my breath. "I told her I'd endure it every day if it meant I could come home to her, but she refused to let me go through it again. Then she married Holt with the promise they'd leave me be."

"Fuck." I hung my head.

"So, son, I didn't question the story because I

believed it, and knowing Mabel, she knew that if Holt found out about you two, that is precisely what would happen to you and…" He cleared his throat. "There's a good chance Holt would go after me, too. So she came up with the only solution that she thought would work, and yeah, as a consequence, another generation had a shit ton of heartache. But in the end, she saved her daughter from being forced to marry a man for his family's money like she had been."

"Smart woman," I muttered.

Dad huffed. "Her daughter is, too."

"She is."

"And she's right. Tad would have gotten what he wanted."

"I know." I lifted my head and captured his gaze. "How do I fix this? How can I erase that hurt and take away her fear?"

He fell back into his chair. "That I don't know the answer to, but I know you'll figure it out."

"Ya know, Pop, Holt is dead."

"I'm aware," he said slowly.

"And Mabel's dad is long gone."

"Know that, too, son." His mouth was tight, probably nothing new… the battling with himself about his past and Mabel was something he had lived with for far too long.

I stood and walked over to him, grasping his shoulder. "See you for dinner tomorrow night?"

"I'll be here."

"Take care, old man."

I left, my heart and mind still on overload. While I really didn't want to give Georgia any time or space, deep down, I realized she needed it. And knowing that she was safe for the night, I gave it to her. But that was it, just one night apart.

CHAPTER 14

Georgia

EVEN THOUGH MY DAD NEVER USED TO BE AROUND that much, his stifling energy was always within the walls of my house, no matter how far away he was. Mom and I only ever seemed to be totally relaxed when we did something in the city, far away from home.

And now that he was gone, it was still kind of... eerie in the house. Like his evil spirit lingered and was just waiting to jump out at me.

My mom had already started boxing things up in preparation to put the house on the market, and I was doing the same in my bedroom. There wasn't much to go through since I took most of my stuff with me when I first left.

"Knock, knock." Mom came in with a bottle of champagne and two glasses. "I thought we could celebrate."

"It's nine in the morning, Mother."

She made a *pshh* sound and handed me the fancy flutes. "It's five o'clock somewhere."

"What are we celebrating?"

"I got an offer on the house."

My eyes widened. "Already? I didn't even know you put it for sale yet."

The cork popped, and bubbles fizzed out onto her hand, but she didn't care. In the days I'd been home, it was clear that she was carefree, and I was happy for her. It made me question myself, and even though I knew I was allowed to feel what I felt, it was difficult to accept that I was relieved my father had a heart attack. What kind of daughter doesn't cry about the demise of the man who she shared her DNA with? However, seeing my mom even more relieved than me made me feel less guilty, so I tried not to be too hard on myself.

"Well, I guess the price was right." She handed me a glass and tapped hers against mine. "To new beginnings."

"To new beginnings, Mom."

She took a big gulp and then topped off the glass before setting the bottle on the floor. "I have an idea."

"What?"

"Let's go have a spa day, just you and me."

"I wish I could, Mom, but I can't." I released a sigh. "I have a tour scheduled for a house at eleven."

She frowned. "You do?"

"I just got the confirmation this morning."

"Is Beau going with you?" she asked.

"I want to go by myself." Because I knew he wouldn't even let me go because he would insist I move in with him. It was like no time had passed between us. Back then, he didn't want us to be apart, so there was no way he'd accept anything less now. "Or you could come with me, maybe you'll like it, and we could live together for a little while." Although I knew the modest size and old-school charm weren't up to her standard. I had the money for something bigger and better, but I actually preferred a smaller place... plus, it was close to town and Beau. And it was a rental. I didn't want to buy anything yet, not knowing what exactly was in store for the future.

She rolled her lips. "For the first time in my life, Georgia, I don't have someone controlling my actions, so I want to enjoy that. I have a suite booked at a hotel in Lawless that has a top-of-the-line spa and restaurant. As soon as I get everything with this house taken care of, I'm going to do nothing but relax while I figure out where I want to go next."

I could respect that. "Okay, I get it."

We sipped champagne and went through some more stuff, and I took off to go to the viewing. The house was pretty close to Beau's childhood home, so driving through the neighborhood was nostalgic.

When I got out, I parked and was greeted by a woman I hadn't seen in years. "Cheyenne?"

"Georgia! Oh my God!" My childhood friend ran over to me, and we gave each other a huge hug. It was so nice to be greeted happily, and I felt tears well in my eyes. "You're back?" She took a step away and held me at arm's length. "Are you really back?"

"I am."

"How long has it been since we last talked?"

I dabbed my cheek with my sleeve to dry up the tears that fell. "It's been a few years, and I don't know how."

"I know, I'm sorry. Life has just been crazy, and I've been swamped. I've missed you, but I'm so excited to see you again."

"I missed you, too. We've got lots to catch up on for sure, and as much as I'd like to right now, I've gotta feed Lucy and get her to an eye doctor's appointment this afternoon."

Of course I knew that she was a mom—we'd stayed close for a long time after I left—but like she said, life just got busy, and we drifted apart over the past few years. "Definitely, we can do it later. You look great, Shy."

She rolled her eyes and simultaneously blew a strand of hair off her face. "I'm a mess. I was in the middle of cleaning when Gage called and told me about the showing, so I had to pull Lucy away from her program and rush here." We stopped on the front porch where Lucy was sitting on the top step. "Lucy, this is Miss Georgia. Can you say hello?"

"Hi, Miss Georgia." She lifted her head from a game she was playing on a phone enough to acknowledge me. She looked just like Cheyenne. Raven hair, shorter, a little plump but you could tell she was strong.

"Hi, Lucy." I tilted my head at Cheyenne. "Wait. How is this *your* house?"

"It's not. I mean, it belonged to Gage's parents' before they passed. He's been renting it out, and the last tenants moved out a few weeks ago. I didn't even know he put an ad out for it. He's been out of town for work a lot lately, so I've gotten stuck doing everything." She quickly shook her head. "Not that I feel stuck showing you the place, it's just—"

"It's okay. I get it."

Her lips flattened. "I'm sorry about your dad."

"Thanks." I smiled. "I appreciate you saying that."

"Well, come on, let's show you the place."

"Sounds good."

Cheyenne opened the front door, and I went in behind. "Water and trash are included. It's a two bedroom, but I'll be honest, the second bedroom is really small, so it's usually used for an office. Gage is still going to put on a fresh coat of paint and the faucet in the kitchen needs to be replaced, too."

I followed her and looked around at the old but updated space, stopping in the larger bedroom. "It's nice. I didn't realize this was where Gage grew up."

"Yeah, I spent plenty of nights sneaking through his bedroom window."

"You did not!"

She waggled her eyebrows. "You weren't the only one with secrets."

"Yeah, but you knew all of mine."

"Speaking of…" She held her hands out expectantly. "Does Beau know you're back?"

"He does." I bit my lip and could feel the flush on my cheeks.

"Oh my God. You slept with him already!"

I covered my face and peeked through my fingers. "It just happened."

"Yeah, okay. Just happened, my ass. I want details later."

"All right, fine." I looped my thumb through my belt loops. "I know you've gotta get going, so let's take a look at the backyard really quick."

"Sure." We went out there and I was surprised to see a rather large yard, probably at least a quarter of an acre. The trees on the side of the house hid how deep the yard went. "Wow. This is really nice."

"Yeah, but we both know you can do better than this, Georgia. So what gives?"

I sucked my teeth. "I want something temporary."

"You can't stay at your mom's place?"

"My mom sold the house already, but even if she didn't, I'm too old to live there. I can afford to be on my own, but I just don't want to invest too much when I don't know where I'll ultimately end up."

"You mean if you're going to end up with Beau?"

"Not necessarily. I mean what if I can't find work here? The clinic is small, and if I go back to a hospital, I've gotta go to Lawless. My mom's moving now., and I want to be close to her...there's. There's just a lot in the air right now."

She reached across her chest and rubbed her bicep. "I get it."

"Good, because I like the place. And I want it. I just...

don't know how long I'll need it for. Do you require a lease?"

"Not for you," she responded quickly.

"But if you can find someone else long-term—"

Lucy stuck her head out the door. "I'm hungry."

Cheyenne pinched the bridge of her nose. "I know, me too, sweetie. We're leaving in a couple of minutes."

"Let's go to the Pig." I offered. "My treat. I'd like to catch up anyway so we can kill two birds with one stone."

"I was going to go there anyway, so I'd love to have you join us."

"Perfect. I'll meet y'all there."

I arrived just before her and was greeted with a big hug from Ms. Lorna. When Cheyenne and Lucy got there, we got a table and ordered right away. I didn't need a menu to know that I wanted some chicken fried steak.

After Lorna brought our drinks, I asked Cheyenne, "So what else have you been up to besides being a mom?"

"Right now, just being a mom and holding down the fort while Gage works. He's been in Louisiana during the week so he's only home on weekends. It's been a little hectic to say the least. What about you?"

"Nothing different from the last time we talked, just working at the hospital."

"Fair enough." She narrowed her eyes at me. "So why did you really come back? Was it because of your dad or because Tad is finally locked up?"

It was nice to talk to her about this because, aside from my mom, she was the only one who knew. "Tad.

My luck would finally turn around, though, when Dad died nearly the same time."

"Now give me all the deets on Beau... You two hooked up, but are you *back* with him?"

"No. It's been a long time, Cheyenne. We can't just pick up where we left off when we were eighteen."

She grinned. "Why not? Y'all loved each other like crazy."

"There's still a lot we need to talk about, an entire past we need to move on from."

Lucy asked for a refill, and Cheyenne told her it was the last one. "I'm sure there is."

"What does that mean?"

She looked over to make sure Lucy was engrossed in something on her phone. "I was here, and I know it was hard for you to talk about so I didn't say much about what went down after you left, but I will now. If they heard that rumors were spreading, one of the Bradford brothers shut it down. I swear I never told a soul about y'all, but that doesn't mean assumptions weren't made. It wasn't until Beau had clearly moved on that talk of y'all being together completely stopped."

I felt my throat tingling at the thought of him with another woman... let alone a lot of them. "Why are you telling me this?"

"Because I know the truth, and you being back... you might hear things. And I just, I want you to know that I did see you two together back then so I know how he looked at you. After you left, he might have been with other women, but they never *had* him, Georgia. You know how people are, I see them staring now, and I don't want you to hear something and have it get in your head and ruin the second chance you both deserve."

Her words cut deep, but it was my fault for how I left him. "I get it. And as much as I don't want to hear it, I appreciate you telling me." I took a sip of my water. "Enough about me. Tell me everything I've missed."

Cheyenne spent the next half hour filling me in on her life and some small-town gossip I'd missed out on. Our conversation was interrupted several times by people I hadn't seen in forever coming over to say hi, so she didn't get into anything too personal or private, which I could sense she wanted to. Something was off about how she talked about Gage, and after I paid the bill, we promised to get together as soon as she had the time.

We exchanged up-to-date contact information and she was going to send me a copy of the lease agreement after she edited it to say month to month. I discovered we both had the same cell number as we did in high school, which struck me like lightning. Beau never had a cell back then, and he'd since moved out of his pop's home and gotten a new number, but mine remained the same after all these years.

She and Lucy walked back to their car, and I stayed behind to use the restroom as unwelcoming thoughts began to muddle my brain. Then I got stuck talking to Ms. Lorna for a bit, which wasn't a bad thing, especially since she gave me a piece of her famous pie. Her daughter and

I were friends growing up and cheered together in high school, so it was good to hear how she was doing since she'd moved away.

When the afternoon rush started, I finally said good-bye and went outside, inhaling the deepest breath of the warm air. I intended to go to my car, but when I saw the sign for The Tap just up the block, I decided to make a detour there.

We'd all heard the stories throughout the years since it was always such a big deal when someone in town turned twenty-one because they could finally go into the bar and drink. Everyone looked forward to it as a rite of passage, and if, for some reason, you left for college or something else, you always tried to come back to celebrate your birthday at The Tap.

I never got to do that, and the last time I was there, I left almost immediately to have it out with Beau in the parking lot.

So I figured I would make up for lost time today. And, honestly, I needed a little time to clear my head. Things had happened so fast, and I knew that Beau wouldn't give me any more space once tomorrow came. Not that I wanted it, but right now, I *needed* it.

"Georgie Peorgie."

I grinned as I made my way to the bar and teased an old friend. "Bobby Bobby."

"I heard you were back."

"You heard right."

He set his rag down and came around to give me a hug. "Glad the rumors were true."

"You look great." I complimented, patting his bicep when he took a step back.

"So do you." He ran his eyes down my body. "Looks like you put on a few, but—"

"Shut up." I smacked him.

He rubbed his arm and chuckled. "But it looks good on you, girl."

Such a ladies' man. "I see you haven't changed at all."

He sauntered back behind the bar and lifted a shoulder. "Only gotten better. What are you drinking?"

"Surprise me."

I hauled my butt up on a stool and watched with wide eyes as he mixed a couple of different liquors and juice, then slid a glass in front of me. "Hurricane. You look like you could use something strong."

"So not only have I gotten fat but I also look like shit?" I quirked a brow as I took a sip.

"I never said that."

I smacked my lips. "Wow. This is good."

"I know." He winked as he wiped down the bar top. "So… I'd say I'm sorry about your dad, but that would be a lie."

"Someone finally said it," I muttered. "Makes sense you'd be the honest one."

"He tried to screw over Jeanie several times over the years when she got into some financial trouble with the bar, but aside from that, he was a dick."

"Yeah." That was something I'd learned after I moved away. My mom told me stories about the shit my dad tried to pull with a lot of the town's small business owners. I didn't know about it since nobody treated me differently because of who he was, but hearing how vindictive he was didn't come as a shock.

"What's the deal with you and Beau?"

I choked on a sip of my drink and he slid a glass of water in front of me that I gulped down to stop coughing. "What?"

"Heard the two of you put on quite the show here the other night—him storming off, you chasing after him."

"We had some things to discuss," I said flatly.

"I bet you did."

I shot him a glare. "What's that supposed to mean?"

He leaned a hip on the ledge where the liquor bottles sat. "Despite what y'all think, the whole town knows about you two, at least everyone around our age. Maybe not the details, but that something was going on. Don't forget we went to the same high school so we saw all the tension between y'all. It was even more obvious when you left, and he was clearly not in a good place. Might have been a long time ago, but it's hard to forget things like that when it involves people like y'all."

"People *like us*?" I asked.

"Yeah. Pretty. Popular."

"What did everyone think? About Beau and me?"

His head tilted to the side. "That it was about time when y'all were spotted together after graduation. That something bad had to have happened for you to leave town so quick. That he was a fool for not going after you. And that it was a shame two people meant to be together... weren't. Just like Maverick and Cricket." He angled his head toward the back of the bar where the Ryder brothers were all sitting in a booth, sharing a pitcher. "Man's never been the same since she left and Beau was almost unrecognizable when you ditched town."

God, nobody knew about Tad. On the one hand, it was good, but on the other, I wanted everyone to know what an asshole he was. "Tad beat me up." The words rolled off my tongue before I knew what I was saying. "He threatened Beau." And they just kept coming. I told Bobby everything, and as I did, I watched his facial expressions change from anger to sadness, to more anger. He handed me another drink, and I practically slammed it before he gave me a third. I didn't know what was happening or why I felt the need to confess my darkest secrets, but I did.

"I always knew Tad was a prick, but I just had no clue how much. Jesus, Georgia, an arranged marriage. What the fuck?"

"I know, I wouldn't believe it was real unless I lived it. But Bobby, please don't tell anyone. I don't need pity from everyone, not when I'm trying to start over."

He reached over and gave my hand a squeeze, and said, "Cross my heart, Georgie Peorgie."

"Thanks, Bobby Bobby."

It started to get busy, and as I looked around, I began

to miss Beau. No, not miss him. I *craved* him. I wanted to go home to him. I didn't want time to think. I didn't want to live somewhere else while we got used to each other again and made sure it was right.

I never wanted anything but Beau Bradford, but the longer I was home and the more people I talked to, I questioned just how much he wanted me. He never called, never came to see me, didn't bother fighting for me. Although my mom's story to him was convincing and held a lot of truth, I thought what Beau and I had was special enough for him to at least try to reach out. Maybe it was the alcohol, but I was starting to question if my being back was really what he wanted.

And there was only one way to find out.

CHAPTER 15

Beau

"**H**EY, MAN. YOU MIGHT WANT TO GET DOWN here."

Grumbling, I settled into my couch. Not only was I off tonight, but unless it was Georgia, I didn't want to see a single soul. I was too busy brooding about what she said, pissed off beyond belief that she could ever even think that she didn't have every single part of me there was to give. She'd always had it all. I understood being confused and wanting space, but after so much time apart, I was beyond ticked that she wanted to spend the night away from me. "I'm off today, Bobby. Call dispatch."

"I would, but I think you'll want to be the one to deal with this."

"Deal with what?" I sat up and pressed the phone harder to my ear as the noise from the bar was drowning out his voice. If Baker got into another fight, I was tempted just to leave him there and have him sleep it off in a cell. Maybe then he'd learn his lesson.

"Well…it'd seem that Georgia's had a few too many, and by the looks of things, the cowboy who's been hittin' on her all night is trying to get her to leave wi—"

"Do not let her outta your sight. I'm on my way."

Word spreads fast in a small town, and all it took was someone seeing her get in my truck last night and the rest was history. Plus, I was sure Baker opened his mouth. And everyone at the station knew I had it out for Tad, and when I told them what had happened in high school, I was sure they were smart enough to know there was something between Georgia and me.

Nobody really knew that Georgia and I were together back then. She wasn't aware of it, but a few people did see us out together, and there were rumors. And rumors in a small town were usually nothing but the truth. I never hid how I felt about her throughout high school, so it didn't surprise me that Bobby assumed her being back and us leaving the bar together meant that I was her man, or at least the man who'd take care of some asshole who thought to touch her.

Which I was.

And as such, I needed to go claim her in front of the whole town once and for all.

The smartest way to go about that would have been to throw on my badge and diplomatically inform this guy that the lady was too intoxicated to make decisions, and as I was an officer of the law, it was my duty to make sure she got home safely. But I wasn't feeling very diplomatic.

Not after last night... or this morning, rather. Both, really.

How had she gone so long without a man between her legs was beyond me. Not only was she fuckin' gorgeous but she was a woman, and last I checked, women had needs, too.

I swear, it felt like the first time sinkin' inside her again... and in reality, I guess it kind of was. All I'd thought about all day was how I wanted to relive that experience over and over again. I wanted to go to sleep feelin' her beside me, I wanted to hold her in my arms and know she was safe all night, and I wanted to wake up every morning for the rest of my damn life looking at her hair fanned out on the pillow next to me.

And I knew she wanted to be there, too.

So why was she using some lame-ass excuse to push me away? Why was she running from me? *Again*?

Well, fuck this. I'd waited for her for ten damn years, and now that I finally had her back, I was going to prove to her that if she ran, I'd chase her. And then I'd catch her and wouldn't let her go.

Sliding my feet into a pair of boots, I grabbed my keys and hopped into my truck, loving how her scent lingered from just driving home with me once. I drove faster than I should have, but every second she was there was another second she was in danger of getting hurt by some drunk asshole.

The parking lot was packed, but I stopped and park illegally, knowing I wouldn't get towed. Jumping out, I stomped toward the entrance and twirled my keys around a knuckle as I scrutinized the place to find her. As soon as I saw her, sitting in a seat at the bar with some moth- erfucker leaning next to her and caging her in, *touching her hair*, I tucked my keys into my pocket and marched across the dance floor.

"I'm gonna have to ask you to remove your hands and step away."

Georgia's spine snapped straight, and she turned around, *in his fucking arms,* and stared at me. Looking part shocked, part irritated, part relieved, but mostly accept- ing that she was mine now and understanding what being with me meant. Nobody got their hands on her but me.

He slid his fingers from her hair and down, letting it rest on the small of her back, and my fists twitched. "I'm gonna have to deny your request. You want a piece, you can have it when I'm done, but I saw her first."

"That's gross." she spat, narrowing her eyes in disgust. Then she started to get up, but he pressed down so she flopped back into the seat.

I was mad before, even livid thinking about what I would be walking into, but seeing it had stirred up a fero- cious rage that had been in hibernation for way too long. "I won't tell you again. Let her go and step away."

He shifted against her, slithering his finger beneath the waistband of her jeans, when she drunkenly protested, "Don't touch me, asshole."

And then I totally lost it. I hadn't lost it in a long time. I was actually well controlled visiting Tad, which surprised Grayson. The last time my control snapped was probably when Tad was assaulting her, and then again after she left. But those were for two very different reasons; however, they were both because of her. She pushed me past my own world and into a place where life was centered around her, and the possibilities were infinite but the consequences could be catastrophic.

When she tilted her head up to glare at the guy, he glanced down at her, and I took the opening and jabbed him with my left hand, then grabbed his arm and twisted his wrist with enough force to break it. He howled out in pain and released her as he tried to free himself from my hold.

She lurched to the side, crying out and almost fell off the stool. But I reached out to steady her, all the while twisting harder on his arm and bringing him to his knees with a thud. "Fuck, dude. Shit." He cursed and bellowed, and if it wasn't for the crowd, I'd have kneed him in his face just to teach him a lesson. But unfortunately, I couldn't do that.

Instead, I let him go and wrapped my arm around Georgia's waist and led her out of the bar. I tossed her on the bench seat of my truck. "Are you okay?" I asked, holding her face in my hands. Some motherfucker touching her like that probably brought back memories of Tad.

She nodded shakily. "I'm good."

I sighed and kissed her jaw, then skirted around to my side. Her eyes closed almost immediately, and her only noise was a cute little whistle when she breathed.

Some of my anger dissipated on the short drive back to my place, and by that time, she was pretty much passed out. I carried her inside and laid her on my bed, watching to make sure she didn't roll off.

I'd never seen her drunk before, so I wasn't sure if she was a puker, but I grabbed the trash can from the bathroom and put it by the side of the bed just in case. Then I took off her shoes and tugged her shorts off, leaving her in her sexy as fuck, barely-there underwear. A wave of nostalgia hit me when I pulled my old flannel down her arms. "My favorite shirt," she mumbled, and I wished she wasn't so wasted so I could fuck her to let her know how much it means to me that she kept a piece of me with her all these years.

I wasn't about to leave her alone, so I chucked my pants off and took off my T-shirt, then went to lie next to her.

Staring at the ceiling, I listened to her breathe and didn't think I'd be getting any sleep tonight. After only a couple of minutes, she groaned a little bit and then rolled over. I prepared to grab her when she started throwing up, but all she did was continue rolling until she cuddled against me.

"What do you know about hurricanes?" she asked against my chest.

I tilted my head down. "What?"

"Bobby made me some. They tasted like juice, but they got me drunk."

"Yeah, they did." I chuckled. "All I know about

them is there's a lot of liquor in them, too much for you, apparently."

"I wanna see you drunk."

"Why?"

She walked her fingers up my chest and then tickled my neck, or at least tried to. "You're still not ticklish."

"I never will be."

"Never?" she whined.

"No, Gigi, I don't think that changes as someone gets older."

She tried to prop herself up on her arm but missed and head planted into my shoulder. "Ouch."

"What are you doing?" My chest shook as I moved her back where she was.

"I wanted to look at your face."

"Why?" I asked.

"Because somehow you got hotter, and it's not fair."

I ran my fingers down her spine. "No, what's not fair is that you got even more beautiful."

"I got fat. Bobby said so."

"He *what*?" I tilted her chin up until her glazed eyes met mine. "What did he say?"

"I put on a few, and he's right." She rolled off me and dramatically threw her arm over her face. "I can't help it that I like to eat, Beau. Food is fuel, and you need it to keep you alive, so it should at least taste good, right?"

My lips were in a flat line until she finished her rant. "Right. And Gigi, I hate to break it to you, but Bobby was joking."

"He was?" she gasped.

"Yes." I laughed. "You're beautiful. And your body is smokin' hot."

"I'm cold. Hold me."

"Whatever you want." I scooted over and wrapped her up in my arms. "Anything else?"

She sighed. "No. You showed up tonight. That was all I wanted, for you to fight for me."

My laughter died, and her weight got heavy. And as I held her, I stared at the ceiling, thinking once again that I wouldn't be getting any sleep tonight.

CHAPTER 16

Georgia

I N THE BACK OF MY HEAD, BETWEEN THE THROBBING and dizziness, I knew where I was. And I also knew what I did. I just didn't know why I did it. I was too old to play games, and Beau and I had been through enough. The last thing we needed was me being stupid to risk what we were trying to rebuild.

"Sleepy." I pried open my eyes to find Beau standing next to the bed, grinning, looking down at me. "You're a sleepy drunk. I always wondered what you'd be like with a little alcohol in your system."

"I'm sorry, I—"

"Don't apologize, Gigi. It's okay."

"Do you have any ibuprofen?"

He held out his hand, and halos appeared above a couple of tablets. "Water." I took the bottle he offered as well and guzzled half of it, then set it on his nightstand before lying down again.

"You've been through a lot, and I understand your

head is messed up. This is all happening fast, and it's scary and confusing. We're gonna have bumps in the road, and I'm here for it. But what you did last night? That shit doesn't fly. Never again, you hear me?"

"I was embarrassed," I confessed in a whisper. And me going to a bar and getting wasted, knowing someone would call him to come and get me seemed like a good idea at the time. But my behavior was even more mortifying than the reason I was embarrassed in the first place.

"About what?"

"It's kind of pathetic that I'm a born-again virgin." I swallowed the burning humiliation and powered through. "I forced myself to be busy to try to forget about you, and by the time I thought I was ready to even go on a date again, nobody compared to you, and I couldn't bring myself to go there."

He dipped his chin to his chest. "Sucks you didn't get off, but… and it's gonna make me sound like a dick, but I'm glad, because for me, it's fuckin' awesome."

I turned my head on the pillow, and he sat down by my legs.

"Really?"

"Hell, yes. Not just because you're unbelievably tight, which means all good things for me, but more than that, it does something to a man, knowing his woman didn't spread her legs for anyone else, that he's the only one who knows how beautiful she is on the inside, too. And I know you'd say the same could be true if the roles were reversed. But I want you to understand that not one of the chicks I've been with had more than a few hours of my time. You've had all of me forever, Georgia. That's what's important."

I hated thinking about him with other women. And it wasn't like I never had the opportunity. I just didn't want it. "Okay."

"I know all of this is scary. Between the reason you left and why you came back and everything else, it's been rough. I'll do whatever I need to—I'll assure you however much you need to hear it, make love to you as many times as you need to feel it, and prove every time I'm tested that I love you. Only you. And I swear I will until the day I die."

Crying with a hangover headache sucked. But the reason the tears were rolling down my temples made any of the pain I'd gone through worth it. "I love you, too."

"I know you do."

"I missed you so much it hurt every single night I went to sleep alone. Every day I woke up without you. Something would be on the news that I wanted to talk to you about, and I couldn't. Or I'd have a bad day at work and want nothing more than to come home to you and have you make it better because you did. You always made everything better." Even when I was pretending to hate him, whenever he'd say my name the rest of the world would just melt away, and it did something to me, knowing he was there. "And I knew back then that you loved me, and now... there's still something there, but you never... you didn't try to get me back once. And I thought that meant you didn't want me at all anymore, so I never even tried to reach out to you."

He reached out and stroked a hand down my back. "I was young and dumb, baby. Completely powerless against your father. I wasn't independent yet and had responsibilities. I thought about it. So much. And I always told myself that once I was confident I could keep you safe, when I finally made Tad pay for what he did, when I knew I could protect you from your dad, I'd have a reason for you to come back since I wasn't enough to make you stay." His chin went to his chest. "You just beat me to it, Gigi."

"You were going to come to me?" I said in awe.

"I was."

My heart swelled and a shuttering breath moved through my lips. "I didn't know that."

"Well, now you do. And I'm here and I'm not going anywhere, neither are you. You don't have to worry about that again. It took a decade, but I can finally fucking say, you don't have to worry about anything anymore."

Sighing, I rolled over to my back, and he wiped away the wetness before it fell to my cheeks. "That's not true," I countered, not wanting to bring Tad into his bed but needing to talk about it.

"It is."

"It's not."

He tilted his head. "Wanna bet?"

"I'm scared for what's going to happen when he gets out," I whispered. "I hate being scared, and I don't want to do it anymore."

"I know you don't, so let me prove to you that you don't have to be anymore. I can take care of you, I can protect you, I will shield you from him, and I promise to guard your heart while I'm doing it." His jaw clenched. "He'll never get close to you, and he might be an arrogant piece of shit with money, but he's not dumb. He's not gonna even try to fuck with me now. He lost, baby. We won. Let's celebrate the victory instead of dwelling on the possibility of more defeat."

My head was a little achy, but other parts of me ached more. I scored my nails down his bare back, and his pupils dilated. "I know how we can celebrate."

"Yeah?"

My fingers teased him as they reached their destination beneath the elastic of his boxer briefs, and the muscles in his abdomen contracted. "Yeah."

"You don't feel shitty?"

"I feel a lot of things right now, Beau."

He lay on his side next to me, his head propped up with his bent arm, and his leg thrown over mine, caging me in. I shivered as he trailed the tips of his fingers up my thigh, past my hips, around my breasts, then he swiped a thumb across my nipple, and my back arched. "I do, too, honey. I feel this." He pinched the tight bud and rolled it before ghosting down my stomach. Knowing where he was headed caused a rush of moisture to dampen the cotton covering me. "I see that," he growled. "Can smell it, too."

"*Beau...*"

Instinctively knowing what I was asking for, just by saying his name, he sat up, stripping me of my thong. Then he settled between my legs and ran a knuckle between my folds, barely touching me, driving me wild. When he got to my clit, he pressed his thumb down and circled it. Waves of ecstasy flowed through me and my hips shot up involuntarily, but he pushed them down. The second my backside was back to the mattress, he thrusted a finger inside me. "I feel this, too. Feel how tight you are, how wet your pussy is, how fuckin' pretty you are down here." He continued the torture—teasing, toying, and all I could do was lay there and take it. "I wanna feel you when you come for me, Georgia. Can you do that?" He thrusted deeper and circled harder. "Can you come for me?"

"Yes," I cried out as an explosion of sparks and fire blasted through me, my thighs trembling, toes curling at the primal act of possession. But I loved it. God, did I love it.

"Fuck, Gigi. That's so hot." My head was tossed back, and my eyes were closed as I focused on the delicious sensation of what he could do to me, so I didn't see him move, but I felt his mouth between my legs.

"Holy shit," I panted and grabbed his hair, pulling him deeper but at the same time pushing him away. Wanting more but was hyperaware that it could destroy me.

He licked from my hole to my clit, then back down, then wrenched his mouth away. "Felt it all, now I'm gonna taste it, then you're gonna feel me, Gigi, right after you taste me too."

God, yes, I loved sucking his cock almost as much as feeling him inside me. "Yes, please. Now." I reached for him but he shackled my wrist and held it immobile. "Stay still, while I eat you, baby. Then you can wrap those lips around my cock."

"Oh... kay," I dropped my thighs open more, and his chest rumbled as he went down on me.

"So sweet," he murmured, eating and sucking like I was the most delicious treat he'd ever had. "God, I missed this."

"Me, too." I ran my free hand through his hair and tightened my hold, forcing him to look up at me. "I missed you."

He kissed the juncture of my thigh, then crawled up between my legs and thrust inside. His fingers twisted with mine and he raised my arms above my head and dropped his forehead, staring down into my eyes. "I missed you, too."

And then he made love to me. It was slow and gentle until he couldn't take anymore, then it was fast and hard. But it was beautiful. We came together and he collapsed on top of me and as I was running my hands up his back, I kissed his neck, then moved my lips to his ear. "I didn't get to suck your cock."

He shook above me and pushed up, playfully biting my jaw. "Give me ten minutes and I'll be happy to oblige."

It only took five before he was hard again, and after I blew him in the shower, he fingered my clit until I came, never receiving without giving.

∽

"Why did you become a cop?"

He huffed out a breath. We were back in bed after eating breakfast, having a lazy day and just getting to know each other again. It didn't feel like much time had passed, but the reality was that it did, and I wanted to know everything. "It was the only way I could think of to get back at your dad and Tad."

"My dad?"

"Yeah. Remember I was told he was the reason you left? And after that, he actually stayed pretty clean, so unfortunately, I could never find anything good enough to bring him in. He knew I was watching him, and just the fact that it scared him a little made it worth it."

I hated that he was doing something he didn't like just because of all this bullshit. "Do you even like your job?"

"I do. Actually, I love it."

"I'm glad. You're sexy in your uniform." God, remembering seeing him the first time with his cargo pants and tight shirt with a gun belt... I was surprised I was even able to talk. I lied to him about not knowing he was a cop, but as soon as my mom told me he was, all I could picture was how hot he'd be. And I was right. But in person was way better than my dreams.

His fingers flexed. "You're sexy no matter what you wear... or don't."

"I bet you write a lot of speeding tickets."

"Why would you say that?" he murmured.

"The women of Warrenville trying to find any excuse they can to get close to Officer Bradford."

He chuckled. "What about you? Tell me about being a nurse."

"It's a good job. Rewarding. And I liked all the people I've worked with."

"Do you want to go back to work?" My cheek was on Beau's chest, and I tilted back and saw the underside of his sharp jawline. He peeked down and raised a brow when I didn't answer. "Do you?"

I had a nice nest egg from saving. Plus... I had the trust from my mom's side of the family but I hadn't even touched it and I planned on keeping it that way so I could give it to my kids. "I kind of have to, don't I? I mean, I need to eat. I have to pay Cheyenne rent."

"*What*?"

"Yesterday, I looked at a house that Shy and Gage own. She said she'd do month to month and—"

"First, you're not finding another place to live because you're in it right now. This is your home, and you know it, so don't say stupid shit like that. Call Cheyenne and tell her to rent it to someone else, or I will." I opened my mouth for a rebuttal, but he didn't let me. "Second, you're loaded, so I know as much as you do that you don't have to work if you don't want to. Which means my question hasn't changed—do you want to go back to work?"

If I gave him the answer I really felt, he might think it was too fast. But I also didn't want to lie to him.

"Babe." He scooted and rested his back against the

headboard and pulled me astride him. "Stop working yourself up to say whatever it is you're afraid to say and just say it."

I forgot that he knew me so well. "I liked my job as a nurse. It was rewarding helping people. But I really just want to have babies. It's all I ever wanted… to get married and have a house full of kids running around. I want to be there when they get home from school and be able to go into the classroom and help decorate for parties and stuff. My mom never did any of those things, and I always said I would because I knew how much I wanted her to be around when she wasn't." A muscle in his cheek twitched, and I panicked. Was that a bad twitch, a good one, or one where he was trying to keep his mouth shut so he didn't hurt my feelings with his answer? I tried to crawl off him, but he clamped his arm around my waist. "Let me go."

"How many?"

"What?" I froze, and he repeated the question.

My mind was reeling, and I couldn't form an answer because I'd never thought I'd get to be with him, let alone make babies with him. Dreamed of it? Fantasized? Hell, yeah. Thought it would really happen? Nope.

"Are you on the pill?"

I managed to shake my head.

"Well…" He raised a brow. "It might happen sooner than you were planning."

"Oh my God." I didn't even think about that. "You didn't use protection."

The lightheartedness of his statement was already forgotten, and his voice got low and his concentration solely on me. "I'd never put you in jeopardy, your health or your body, so let's get that out of the way, okay?" He rolled through the sentence without giving me time to really comprehend what he said. "As soon as I knew I had you back, there was no way I was having *anything* between us. Nothing. And the reason I want all of you in every way I can get you is because I want that too. Babies. Lots of them. I want this house full of kids and a beautiful woman to come home to. And I need all that to be with you."

I stared into his eyes, at his face, wishing I could do it forever because he was so handsome. "Five."

"What?"

"You have four siblings, and I always thought it was so cool that there were five of you. So the answer is five. I want five kids."

"With me?" He smirked.

I nodded and giggled, then pressed my lips to his happily, but the moment my tongue touched his, all bets were off. He shifted his hips and hardened beneath me, and I pulled away in shock. "*Again* already?"

We were barely dressed, me in his T-shirt and him in a pair of boxers, so it wasn't difficult for him to reach between us and find where he needed to be. I fell down,

. he pushed up, and just like that, I was full of him again. Complete. I was home.

"Yeah, baby. Again already." He lost the humor and encouraged me to move, gliding me up and down, stroking his cock with my body. "Always ready for you."

CHAPTER 17

Beau

GEORGIA SAT ON THE KITCHEN COUNTER WHILE I made us lunch, and I listened to her talk about everything she'd done since she left. There was a lot of focus on her job, since that took up most of her time, but she didn't mention much of her parents at all.

"Tell me about your mom."

"What do you want to know?"

I carried our plates to the big table I had in my kitchen and I sat in my normal spot at the head and she directly to my right. "Well, you haven't said a lot about her at all. Or your dad."

"Not much to say, you pretty much know everything."

"I only know what you told me."

"Well, Mom said he was more miserable than ever, but he pretty much left her alone. She thinks him seeing me beat up woke him up at least a little bit."

I took a drink of my water. "If he was leaving her alone so much, why didn't she just divorce him?"

ANNA BROOKS

"I told her to a million times, but she said she wanted to keep an eye on him to make sure he left me alone."

I coughed as I swallowed and hit my chest. "Damn." I took another sip to clear my throat. "I wasn't expecting that."

"What *were* you expecting?"

"Truth?"

She tilted her head. "Of course."

"Even knowing what happened between her and my dad, I kind of judged her for staying with your dad and allowing his abuse."

"Honestly, I did too. Until I knew everything. Like you, she felt powerless and was just waiting for the right time. She feels bad about what I went through, but she knew she had to be smart and that it was going to take time to get ahead of him, but all along her goal was to get me out of here."

I blew out a frustrated breath. "I get that, but also, you were a kid getting slapped around by your father Gigi, and I hate to say it, but she left you alone all the time to deal with him on your own."

"Not really. I mean, yeah, she left me alone, but it was rarely, if ever, when he was home."

I took a bite of my sandwich and must have had a look on my face.

"Just say what you want to say, Beau."

"I didn't know about him physically hurting you

214

until we got together. She lived with that for God only knows how long—"

"I don't need God to tell me how long, Beau, because I was there. And the first time was when I was nine but I talked back so I thought I deserved it. I remember him hitting her as early as five years old, and you're right, she lived with it. *She lived with it.* She didn't have many choices back then because *my* dad made hers look like a saint and she was scared. You have no clue what it's like to live in fear all the time and—"

I reached over and put my hand on hers. "Okay, babe. I'm sorry. I get it."

"Do you?" she snapped.

"Yeah. And you're right. She was the one who had to endure and she did the best she could."

"Just like you felt helpless in the months we were together, imagine how she felt for years not being able to protect me. And when he was gone on a trip, she took that time to have some peace for herself, and I didn't and don't blame her for anything my father did."

I grabbed the leg of her chair and pulled her closer to me. "You've made your point. I shouldn't have said anything."

"No, you should have, but now that you know I hope you can understand and not think she's a terrible mother."

I stroked a hand through her hair. "I never thought she was that."

"She did her best."

"I know, Georgia," I murmured.

Her eyes darted over my face and she sighed. "I suffered less than her and my kids won't ever have to know what it's like feeling unsafe in their own home, so in the end it all worked out."

"*Our.*"

"What?"

"You said my kids. They're gonna be our kids, babe, all five of them."

Her lips kicked up on the sides. "Our kids."

"One last thing." I rubbed my thumb across her hand. "There are two people it still hasn't worked out for, and I think it's time we do something about that."

∽

"Wow, she isn't wasting any time, is she?" I muttered as I pulled behind a moving truck in the driveway. There were a bunch of guys carrying out boxes and it looked like one truck was already filled with furniture.

"I told you she was ready to move on."

I got down and opened her door, then took her hand as we went inside. "Damn," I whistled, seeing the place almost completely bare. I'd never been in her childhood home, and it was even larger than it looked from outside.

"Oh, hi, y'all." Mabel lifted her head from a paper she was signing and approached us with a huge smile on her face. I'd seen her around town often, and never once did I see her genuinely happy. "You two look perfect together! This is so great!"

She clapped her hands together and hugged us both.

"Mom, stop. That's embarrassing," Georgia protested.

"Oh hush, it's true."

"She's right. We do look good together, babe."

"Whatever," Georgia rolled her eyes. "So... I see the movers came."

Mabel nodded enthusiastically. "They're almost done and are coming back to take whatever you don't want from your room. I know most of your things are still in storage from what you brought down from Chicago, but you've got a couple of weeks before the new owners get the keys, so take your time."

"Okay, I'll go do that now. I'm going to be moving in with Beau, so I'll just take my stuff to his house."

"Our house."

She grinned. "*Our* house."

"That sounds perfect, dear."

"What are you doing for supper tonight, Mabel?" I asked.

She scrunched her brows. "I'm not sure yet, but I'll figure it out."

"Join us at my dad's."

Georgia and her mom shared many similar features, but when Mabel's face flashed in horror, I recognized the pain and I didn't like it. "Oh. No... I can't."

"Why not?"

"Because... because it's not... he, I... I just can't."

I wasn't backing down. "Dad would love to see you, Mabel."

"I think I should wait and—"

"You've waited nearly half your life, so has he. There's nothing stopping either of you." And if she didn't take the bait and come tonight, then I'd force my dad's hand to make a move.

Her eyes got glassy and she cleared her throat and sniffled as she stood straight. "I might be able to. Um... what time?"

"We're heading over at six."

"All right, maybe I'll see you then. Oh, shoot, that was supposed to stay." She ran off after a mover and Georgia took my hand and pulled me up the steps to her room.

As soon as we were inside, she closed and locked the door, then dropped to her knees. "What are you doing?"

"Something I fantasized about when I laid in that bed and touched myself."

My cock sprang free when she lowered my jeans and I was already hard for her. Christ, she did it for me without even touching me. Her lips wrapped around me and she sucked deep. My head hit the door and I groaned. "Fuck, Gigi. Fuck."

Her fingers caressed my balls while she worked my dick and I let her play until I couldn't take it anymore.

Then I fisted her hair and held her still while I fucked her face. Movers were making noise on the other side of the wall and I saw her excitement when they stopped just outside her door and talked about taking a break for lunch. My knees started to shake and I pulled her off me then reached down and picked her up and tossed her on the bed. Working my cock with my hand, I cupped her face with the other one and slid my thumb in her mouth. "Show me how you touched yourself."

She sucked hard and I grunted, watching her kick her shorts off and pushing her panties to her ankles. Her pussy was dripping and she dipped a finger inside, then spread all that delicious nectar to her clit and began to circle.

"Fuck yeah." I encouraged. "You're so fucking hot, baby. Make yourself come."

Her legs opened wider and she added her other hand to the party, and started to fuck herself with her own fingers. Her hips rocking with her movements and her moans getting louder.

I jacked myself harder, faster, sliding my thumb out of her mouth and my hand into her hair so I could tilt her face up and give her head a little shake when her eyes started to lower. "Watch me, Georgia. Watch how fucking hard you make me. Do you see that?" I turned her head and rubbed the tip of my cock against her lips. "Feel that. Taste it. Christ, that's all for you, baby." She opened wide and I slid into her willing mouth, and when I hit the back of her throat she reached up and took hold of me, then started bobbing her head.

I brought my hand between her legs and slapped her clit, and then thrust three fingers inside her slick heat, and with just the pressure of my palm circling her, she cried out. Her whimpers sounded muffled with my dick in her mouth, and when I felt her pussy clamp tight on my fingers, I shot down her throat.

My knees gave out and I sat on the edge of her bed, slowly working my fingers as she came down, and when she finally relaxed and opened her eyes, she smiled. "I like your ideas better than mine."

And then I dropped my head and laughed so hard I couldn't breathe. "God, Gigi. I love you."

"I know. I love you, too."

While Georgia was helping her mom and going through the rest of the stuff from her room, I left her and met Bear and Brock at her storage unit. Baker didn't answer his phone so I left him a long message explaining everything so he wouldn't be a dick tonight. "Thanks for doing this y'all."

"No problem."

"Anytime."

I unlocked the lock and lifted the door, surveying her belongings she brought down with her. "She told me it wasn't much." I chuckled as I looked at the jam-packed unit.

"Eh, it probably looks worse than it is," Bear said. "Should only take us a couple of trips."

"All right. If y'all need to get back to work then just do one load and drop the key at my place, otherwise I'll just get it back tonight."

"We can get it all done in a couple of hours, man."

"Thanks, Brock."

He clasped me on the shoulder. "We're real happy she's back."

"Good 'cause she's not goin' anywhere. And I think to understand why I won't let anything stand in our way this time, y'all need to know the truth…"

CHAPTER 18

Georgia

I WAS STANDING IN FRONT OF THE BATHROOM MIRROR, straightening my hair after taking another shower with Beau. He'd already gotten dressed and was waiting for me to finish so we could go to his dad's for supper tonight. I was nervous to see his family again. When I returned just a couple of days ago, I didn't expect everything to happen so fast, so I was unprepared to come face-to-face with them.

With the history and everything, I knew the Bradfords probably resented me, and I hated that as much as I understood it. I wished I had a bunch of siblings who loved me and had my back, so I couldn't begin to hold their anger against them. But the fact that Brock and Bear helped move all my stuff this afternoon gave me hope that I was forgiven for hurting Beau.

"Tell me about your brothers. What they're all doing now and stuff."

"'Kay, let's go down the list. Did you know Brody moved?"

Wow, I never would have thought any of them would have left this town. "No. I had no clue." It was so painful to talk about Beau that whenever my mom tried to bring him or anyone from his family up, I shut the conversation down immediately, so I really didn't know what was happening with any of them.

"He lives in California and works for a big-ass security firm out there. He's actually a bodyguard."

"Wow, that's awesome."

"Yeah, he's happy. Next is Bear. He just graduated from college with his business degree and is kind of figuring out what he wants to do now. Brock is the manager at the shop. And then there's Baker."

I finished gliding the iron through a chunk of hair and lifted my eyes to the mirror. "What's up with him?"

"He's still young, and since he just turned twenty-one, he's partying a lot. Only doing the bare minimum at the shop. Getting into all sorts of trouble." His jaw tensed. "I've tried talking to him, but he's not receptive to anything I have to say. He just blows me off like I'm overreacting."

"Are you?" I asked gently.

"No. There's a difference between having a good time and being reckless."

Damn. "Do you think it's just a phase?" I wouldn't know from experience since when I was twenty-one, I was drowning in schoolwork and lived a totally anti-social life.

He sighed. "I sure as hell hope so."

"And how's your dad been?"

Beau shrugged. "The same, really. Just getting slower as the years go on, but otherwise, he's just like he was ten years ago. I'm hoping I'll see a little pep in his step tonight, though."

I was worried about the answer, but I needed to know. "Do they all hate me?"

"No."

"Not even Baker?"

"No," he repeated.

"But you said me leaving destroyed him."

"It did," he acknowledged. "He loved you. And not that you aren't loveable on your own, but a lot of it had to do with Mom dying shortly before you came into his life. He was missing her and clung to you, so it was like another death to him when you left."

"I can't tell you again how sorry I am for hurting him." I dropped my head so my hair covered the side of my face.

"I know you are, baby. It's time you forgive yourself."

I sighed. Maybe he was right but would I ever be able to banish the guilt completely? "I saw him at the bar. All of y'all that night. Your brothers didn't seem too happy that I was back."

He exhaled behind me, the warm swoosh of air tickling my neck. "They are, Georgia, because you make me happy. That's all they care about."

"Does Baker know the truth? Do any of them know?"

"Bottom line, Gigi, I loved you. And I genuinely

thought the decision you made was the safest for you, that it was the best alternative for an impossible situation. So when you left, I didn't trash-talk you to them. I told them you left because it was best for you and your future. If Baker listens to his voicemail, he'll know what I told Bear and Brock at your storage unit earlier, which was everything."

"And what did they say?"

"They were mad on our behalf, babe. And if they didn't want us together or held a dumb-ass grudge, they wouldn't have helped move your shit."

My lips formed a small opening as I slowly released a pent-up breath. "Okay." I could deal with that. I was just worried they wouldn't want Beau and me to be together, and supper would be awkward.

"You almost done?" He stood behind me and brushed the hair off my shoulder, then nipped at the sensitive skin beneath my ear. "Because if I have to sit here and look at your ass in those jeans any longer, we're gonna be late."

As much as I wanted to entertain the idea of what he had in mind, I refused to be late tonight. "I'm almost done." I shut the iron off and then reached for my mascara to apply another coat, but he took hold of my wrist.

"You don't need that shit." He gave my arm a shake, and I dropped the tube. "Let's go."

He practically dragged me out of the house and once we were in his truck driving away, I got more nervous, despite his reassurances. Beau reached over and rested his palm on top of my thigh, tapping his fingers to the beat of the new Reason to Ruin song on the radio.

It had been so long since I'd been home that I didn't realize how close he lived to his dad. I got a stern look when I jumped down from his truck before he opened my door, but I was apparently forgiven when I pushed up on my toes and kissed his cheek.

My belly fluttered with nerves and excitement at being back at the Bradfords' house. I loved being inside these walls and prayed to God that I could have a family one day who grew up with the kind of love this family had for each other.

"Let's go."

I walked in behind Beau but couldn't get a word out because I was too busy crying. I wasn't expecting it to happen, but as soon as I saw Baker, the waterworks just came. He held his arms out, and I walked right into them where he hugged me tightly. I really did think he was going to hate me, especially with the evil looks he was giving me at the bar the other night. I hiccuped but managed to apologize. "I'm so sorry I left you when—"

"Hey, hey." He pulled back and looked into my eyes, his almost exotic amber-colored eyes mesmerizing. Seeing him so grown-up made me realize just how much time had passed. "The only thing that matters is you're back."

"It's not the only thing. You didn't deserve for me to just leave you like that, and I want you to know how genuinely sorry I am. I know Beau's told you, but you need to understand that I honestly felt like I didn't have a choice."

His brows pulled together. "It doesn't sound like you did, and if anything, we should be thanking you for keeping his butt outta the slammer." He tossed his thumb over his shoulder at Beau. "He might be a pain in my ass, but I kind of like having him around now, and back then I needed the bastard."

"Aw." Bear came over and put Baker in a headlock, essentially ripping him away from me. "Are you getting sentimental?"

Brock laughed and then hugged me quickly. "Good to have you back."

"Thank you."

"Yeah, I forgot to say that. Welcome back, Georgia," Bear yelled from the living room where he and Baker were wrestling one another.

"Thanks!" I shouted. "It's good to be back."

Beau settled his hand on my lower back, and I leaned into his strength. And as soon as Wade bellowed from the kitchen that supper was ready, it was like we were back to ten years ago as all the guys pushed each other out of the way to get to the table.

"Hey there, little lady." Wade tipped his head. "You're just as pretty as ever."

"Thank you." I couldn't not hug him, so I walked over to the stove and wrapped my arms around his neck and quietly said to him what I'd wanted to for a decade, when I found out what he went through for my mom. "Thank you. *Thank you* for what you did and what you sacrificed, and I am so, so sorry for what you endured." He knew what I was talking about, and I was assured of that when he jerked in a breath.

He pulled back a little and dropped his hands. "You make my son happy, and when you become a parent, you'll understand how important it is for your children to find that. I'd do it all again if only for him to find you."

I didn't think there was a better man on the planet than Wade Bradford. Except for Beau, but he was the way he was because of his father. "I need to go sit down. Otherwise, I'm going to start crying again."

"We wouldn't want that." He gave my arms a squeeze, and I grabbed the basket of rolls off the counter and set them on the kitchen table, then took a seat between Beau and Baker.

Wade made what appeared to be a delicious roast, but I couldn't bring myself to take a bite yet. I was too nervous for the surprise.

The doorbell rang, and Wade set his fork down. "Who could that possibly be? Brody's not coming home, is he?"

"Nope, not Brody." Beau grinned as he stood and went to open the front door for my mother. I tried to hide my smirk, beyond thrilled this was *finally* happening.

"Hi." I was closest to the hallway, so I could hear him. "I'm so glad you came."

"Hi, Beau. Are you sure this is okay?" She sounded so nervous, and I hated that, but this needed to happen. They'd lost out on more time than Beau and I did, so it was only fair they got their shot at happiness now.

"I'm absolutely positive this is okay, Mabel. Come in."

228

They rounded the kitchen, and Wade set his beer down. "Who was th—" His jaw dropped, and Mom clutched the back of my chair. I tipped my head up and held back tears at seeing that ravaged expression on my mother's face.

"Hi, Wade."

"My Belle…"

Mom sniffled at the nickname, and Beau reached down and nudged my arm, then suggested to all of us at the table, "Why don't we all go for a walk?"

"No." Wade suddenly stood and came around the table. "We will." He held his arm out like a gentleman of his generation, and Mom blushed. "Shall we?"

She reached up and took hold of his forearm. "Yes, please."

Everyone watched them walk away, and once the front door slammed, Baker got to his feet and the air in the room iced over at his anger. "What the hell was that?"

I raised a brow at Beau. "They don't know?" He told me he told them.

"He wasn't there this afternoon when I filled my brothers in, and I'm guessing he didn't listen to his message."

"Someone needs to tell me!" Baker shouted and shoved his chair so hard it hit the table and made my glass of wine tilt. I reached out and grabbed it before it all spilled, but the damage had already been done as the near purple liquid rolled off the table and dripped onto my jeans.

Beau glared at his brother. "Calm down, Baker."

"Fuck calm, what the hell was that?"

Brock handed me a towel, and I silently thanked him as I patted my jeans.

Beau sat down next to me and draped his arm over the back of my chair as he addressed Baker. "The only reason I know what I'm going to tell you is because of what I went through with Georgia."

I watched Baker's face get tighter as Beau told him everything he knew about our parents and their short but tragic love story. "And before you jump to conclusions, Dad loved Mom very much. Mabel may have been his first love, but Mom was his last. He was happy. They were happy together and had a wonderful marriage."

Brock and Bear watched their brothers go back and forth with conflicting emotions on their faces. Baker, on the other hand, was fuming. "That's bullshit." He grabbed his hair as he emitted an unintelligible noise and backed up toward the hallway. "Loved Mom, my ass. He never looked at Mom the way he just did to *her*. Fuckin' liar." He stormed down the hallway and slammed the front door, and Beau dropped his head to the table.

"Well, that was fun," Bear lamented.

Brock lifted his chin at me. "None of that is on you. He's just—"

"A fuckin' asshole." Beau grabbed my chin and turned my head so I focused on him. "Sorry, babe."

"It's okay. He's allowed to be upset. It's understandable."

"I agree, but he doesn't have the right to be a dick to you. I'll deal with him later."

I shook my head and held his wrist. "Please don't. I don't want you two fighting." I already felt so guilty for everything that had happened and for hurting the two of them the way I did, so the last thing I wanted was to be the cause of a riff in their relationship.

"This isn't on you."

It sure felt like it was. "But—"

Gotta say, bro." Bear drew our attention over to him. "Mom was beautiful, and no doubt if she was still alive she'd still be beautiful. But if your woman looks anything like *her mom* at that age, you hit the fuckin' jackpot."

Beau grunted. "I struck gold ten years ago, Bear."

He found a pair of sweats for me to wear, and Brock got the stain out of my jeans, then threw them in the dryer. Apparently, he was a master at stain removal since he was in charge of laundry as a kid.

The four of us went back to eating, and once we were finished and the dishes were all cleared, I changed back into my jeans and returned to the kitchen just as Wade sauntered in, whistling. "Your mother is in her car waiting for you to talk to her before she leaves." He shoved his hands in his pockets and skipped—*yes, skipped*—down the hallway.

The three brothers all threw their heads back and laughed while I stood there, mouth agape. Beau slapped my butt and angled his head toward the front door, then shoved my keys in my palm that his brothers brought back from using at the storage unit. "Why don't you drive with her to get your car from The Tap? Make sure she's all good, and I'll do the same with my dad."

"Oh yeah, I forgot my car was there." I shook some of the fog out of my head and tipped my head back. "That's a good idea. See you at your house?"

"*Home*," he clarified before he bent down and kissed me. "I'll leave in just a few, and then I'll be waiting for you." He kissed my nose. "Hurry."

"I will," I said goodbye to Brock and Bear and rushed outside and slid into the passenger seat of my mom's car. "Can you take me to the diner to get my car?"

"Of course."

She pulled away, and I asked what I already knew the answer to. "I'm taking it things went well?"

She sighed dreamily. "I feel like this isn't real. I can't believe it's happening."

"Well, it is."

"Thank you for encouraging me to come tonight," she said.

"Of course."

She pulled up to the bar and stopped next to my car, then turned to face me. "Do you have any idea how hard it is seeing the love of your life make a family with another woman? Looking at him through a crowd and feeling your knees tingle with the desire you crave for him, but knowing you'll never have him? Watching him laugh and realizing you're not the only one for him, but secretly wishing things could change?" She whispered the words, almost in a daze, and leaned her head against the window. I wasn't sure if she wanted an answer to her questions, but I didn't want to imagine that, so I moved the topic toward happier times. I was so sick of living in the past. "What did y'all talk about on your walk?"

"Nothing and everything. He's going to take me out for breakfast tomorrow morning."

She looked so happy, and I absolutely loved it.

"I had a moment as I was walking up to his door tonight when I looked over my shoulder, worried that someone would see me. I almost turned around, but then I remembered I have nothing to fear anymore." She reached over and pats my leg. "And neither do you honey. We're both free."

"We are," I agreed. "Finally."

We said goodbye, and she waited until I got in my car and then waved as she drove away.

I didn't waste any time pulling out of the lot and was giddy with excitement as I got closer to Beau's house. I was so lost in a trance of glee that I didn't notice a blinding set of lights shining in my rearview mirror until they were too close. They didn't seem to realize their brights were on. "What a jerk." I ducked in my seat to try to avoid the glare, but the SUV didn't get off my ass. "Pass me, asshole." I slowed down, hoping they'd just go around me. And they did. They also slammed on their brakes, and I didn't have enough time to react and crashed into them. "*Shit!*"

My neck jerked violently, and my airbags deployed, punching me in the face with more force than I imagined.

Buzzing sounded all around me, and I tried to blink the bright white spots away to no avail. My door was yanked open, and somebody grabbed my arm and pulled me, but I didn't move far since my seat belt was locked.

I knew I should try to fight, and I wanted to—at least scream or something—but everything was bright and dark and spinning yet moving slowly. So slow that when I watched a knife come at me, I didn't realize it had already sliced through until I saw a drop of blood drip off the sharp tip.

CHAPTER 19

Beau

MY FEET WERE SHOULDER WIDTH APART, ONE hand clamped to the back of my neck, the other with my phone to my ear talking to Mabel. "I dropped her off over an hour ago, Beau."

"Did she say if she was going somewhere before she came here?" I knew she wouldn't. She would have told me, and anywhere she went wouldn't take as long as it had regardless. She was excited to be here, anxious to be back in my bed.

Wasn't she?

She wouldn't run off again, would she? And if she did, was she in danger? Or did she realize she didn't love me, that coming back wasn't what she thought it would be? Fuck, no... she wouldn't do that. Not after all this time.

Something happened to her. I felt it in the marrow of my bones.

"No, she said she was going to your house."

"Call me if you hear from her." I knew she was

panicked, but I couldn't reassure her of anything right now. Especially because Grayson was calling.

I switched lines and braced myself, fearing the absolute worst. "Tell me."

"Fuck, Beau. He's gone. I walked by his cell, and it was cleared out. I don't know how it happened—"

"She's late."

"What? Who?"

I swallowed down the burning acid and took a step off my porch, then another. "*Georgia*. She went with her mom to get her car, and she's late coming home. She was supposed to be here over an hour ago."

"Shit. I'm already on my way, but you've gotta tell me where I'm going."

"You know where I'll be."

I hung up and jumped into my truck, peeling out onto the street and flew to Tad's place. He lived on the other side of town, but instead of a house, he was in the high-end condos that were built a couple of years ago, thanks to a development company.

"Fuck!" I pounded on my steering wheel as raw fear clawed at my chest from the inside out. I'd just promised her he wasn't going to get to her and I'd keep her safe, and I didn't do that.

I'd *failed* her.

I should have called for backup from the station, but nobody would be able to help me like my brother could right now. Not only did Brody work for one of the best security companies in the world, but he knew the players in this game since he grew up here and understood the corruption that took place.

It only took one ring for Brody to answer. "What's up, man? I was ju—"

"Clancy got out, and Georgia was supposed to be at my house over an hour ago. I need you or one of your guys to crack whatever fucking system needs to be fucking cracked to find out where this *motherfucker* is with my girl."

"Georgia's back?"

My tires squealed when I turned the corner. "Yes."

"Well shit, why didn't you tell me? That's awesome, bro. I'm happy fo—"

"Pleasantries later."

"Right." He cleared his throat and went into bodyguard mode. "Any new developments or motives I don't know about?"

Tad had only been behind bars for a few weeks, so nothing should have been new. After he was in for a year, I could see him trying to get out for good behavior or something. But three weeks in on a six-year sentence? No way. "Aside from the fact that Georgia told me the real reason she left was because Tad beat the shit out of her, and I went and paid a visit to him yesterday to express my displeasure with him, then no."

"Jesus fuck. Okay, give me ten. I'll get ahold of Q and see what he can dig up."

I didn't waste another second talking to my brother because that was a second their tech genius could be searching for Georgia. And it just so happened that I was at the high-rise. I parked at the curb and then tore off into the entrance, flashed my badge at security, and hauled ass up the stairs. The elevator was too slow.

My footsteps echoed in the empty stairwell, and when I got to the top floor, I pushed the door open so hard it slammed against the wall and the knob got wedged into the drywall. I didn't follow any rules because now was not the time to play a game. And if getting to her meant I got fired, I could give that first fuck.

My boot cracked the door open as I reached for my weapon tucked into my jeans at the back. A couple of lights were on, but that was it.

I made my way through the condo, and when I got toward the master bedroom, I heard the water running in the attached bath. Could be a decoy, so I walked to the opposite end first, rummaged through the closets and everywhere she could be and found nothing.

Stealthily backtracking, I nudged open the door to his room, but he wasn't in it. So I marched to the attached bathroom, gun drawn, pointing at his head through the glass shower door where he was jacking off. "Where is she?"

"What the fuck!" He scrambled to shut the water off as he screamed.

I used his confusion to my advantage and put my boot through his shower door, the entire panel of glass shattering and raining down onto his marble floor. I didn't hesitate to reach through and grab his throat, then shove him against the wall, my pistol flush with his temple. "Where the fuck is she?"

"Who?"

"You know who, motherfucker."

"I don't know!"

I took the safety off, and he squealed like the little bitch he was. Then pulling him toward me, the tips of my fingers curling around his neck, I slammed him against the tile. "What did you do to her? Where the hellfuck is she?"

He choked and kicked out, his feet slicing on the glass, grasping at my arm and trying to pull me away, but I didn't let up. Years of what I'd held back detonated, and I couldn't let go.

"Remember what I said to you? Do you remember me telling you what I would do if you ever touched a single hair on her head?"

"I... don't... know."

Grayson's hand landed on my shoulder. "Bradford, lay off."

"He knows where she is," I growled.

Tad's lips turned purple, and he tried to shake his head.

"Beau. Let up. *Now.*"

I dropped my hand but didn't move, keeping the barrel on his head even when he started sinking to the floor as he sucked in air. "Where is she?"

"Like I said, I don't know." He held his throat and shook his head. "I didn't even know I was getting out, I swear." He reached up and took the towel Gray handed him and covered his crotch with it. "But I probably know who does."

"Talk."

"Dad." He tilted his head back, his now bloodshot eyes looking directly at me, and it occurred to me that the bruising on his face from me slamming my fist into his face yesterday wasn't dark enough. I should have hit him harder. "He got me out. Makes sense that—"

"You're a decoy," Gray butted in, figuring out this was just a setup. "Henry knew everyone would think it was you who took her, but he did. Where would he take her?"

He winced when he tried to sit up, his foot bleeding from the broken glass. "Man, I can't—"

I pushed his calf down, forcing his heel to dig into the shards even more. Gray called out my name as a warning I was taking this too far. But I didn't give two fucks. "You can, and you will."

"Shit. Okay." I released the pressure, and he pulled his legs up and wrapped both arms around them. "He conducts business at the old paper mill by the river."

"Let's move."

I stepped back but squatted down as I put the safety back on and tucked my weapon into my waistband. "Remember what I said," I warned. He clenched his jaw, and I stood, crunching the fragments that used to be the door to his shower beneath my boots. When I got to the archway, I scowled over my shoulder at him. "I'd get you a broom, but I want you to have to walk all over that glass. I want you to feel every slice so you might be able to understand the depth of pain someone would endure for the woman they love. She's back, Tad, and she's mine. She always has been, and you know it. And I swear to Christ, I'll walk on glass, over fire, through it... I'll sell my damn soul to the devil to keep her safe. Then I'll wake up the next day, with her in my arms, and do it all over again."

My phone rang the second my ass hit the seat in my truck. I answered Brody's call as I turned the engine over. Grayson pulled out right behind me in his vehicle, making calls of his own to the office downtown for backup... Like I should have been doing, too. "What do you got?"

"Q started with how Tad got out, traced that to his dad, then went with his gut and found the old paper mill by the river has a deed in his mother's maiden name." Brody spat the words out fast and concise. "That's all we've got, bro. Q's still digging, trying to find anything else that might help, like a GPS signal or phone ping, but with the little we've got to go on all the way out here in Cali, we're a bit limited at the moment."

"Yeah, Tad just told us. Grayson and I are on our way to the old mill."

"He told you willingly?"

If I wasn't terrified outta my mind for Georgia, I'd have laughed. "Something like that."

"She's gonna be okay. Just make sure you keep your shit so you do—" He cut himself off, and I heard a faint voice in the background. "Shit. That motherfucker." My brother cursed. "Turn around, Beau. Q just got a ping on Henry Clancy's vehicle. And it's not at the paper mill. It's the old garage."

"Dad's old garage?"

"Yup, and the land is in Holt Westbury's name." Even dead that asshole was still haunting me.

"You've gotta be shittin' me." I hung up before he said another word. "That fucking motherfucker." I slammed my hand on the dash as I whipped my truck around. Pedal to the floor, I revved the engine and hauled ass as fast as I could to the outskirts of town.

I called Gray, who was tailing me. "Tad lied. He *was* a decoy, but he played us by sending us to the wrong place. She's not at the mill; she's at my dad's old garage."

"The one that had the fire all those years ago?"

"Yeah, except it wasn't a fire. It was arson."

I rolled onto the gravel with Gray right behind me and stopped at the front of the dilapidated building. It was a miracle it was still standing because the fire was so bad. And the fact that Holt bought the land and kept it there was sick. I never thought about it because I just assumed it was abandoned and nobody wanted to buy the land. Probably just a reminder to my father of what he was capable of.

"Backup's about five minutes out." He met me at

the rear of his vehicle and thew a vest at me. "They were already halfway to the mill, so they had to turn around."

"I'm not waiting." I heard him curse.

"I shouldn't be here right now. I could lose my badge over this."

So could I. I ducked around the side and peered through the cracked frame of an old window. "I never asked you to. I'll understand if you walk away right now."

"I'm not walking away. Just for the love of God, please don't kill anybody."

"I make no promises." I whipped out my gun and took aim, then moved forward.

He took my six, and as soon as I walked through where the bays used to be, I heard Georgia whimpering. God, that was a beautiful sound. That meant she was alive. I had no clue what he wanted from her or why she was here, but I was going to end this shit once and for all.

Because he was so busy waving a knife centimeters from her face, he didn't hear us approaching. "You already ruined all of my plans, and your father folded like a cheap tent when you left and screwed me in ways I do not like to be screwed. And now that he's dead, he's managed to screw me yet again. But you can help with that.

"Your mother has already signed over the profit from the house to you. I want that money. You owe me that fucking money. You will give me what I'm owed. If you don't…" He bent down and put his mouth by her ear. "I'll leave you here and go visit your mother."

I motioned for Gray to come around the other side. He crept over, and then we nodded at each other and took a few steps closer, and I saw all of her. God, she was shaking. Her legs were tied to a chair and her wrists were zip tied together, resting on the table with a pen in her trembling fingers.

He circled her and then leaned over her back. "Sign it."

I advanced, Gray followed suit, and just as we got close enough to see the corners of the room, Tad came limping in through the back of the building with a gun pointed at Georgia. "I've gotta admit, you're a lot smarter than I gave you credit for."

"Too bad I can't say the same."

At the sound of my voice, Georgia gasped and whipped her head around. I couldn't look at her because I knew seeing her beautiful, petrified face would be my undoing.

Henry Clancy stood straight and casually walked around the table and met his son. They stood shoulder to shoulder behind Georgia. Henry cleared his throat. "Now, you've got me in quite the conundrum, folks."

"Yeah, why is that?" Gray asks condescendingly.

"I wasn't planning on killing anybody today, but you've left me with no choice." I saw it in slow motion, Henry's grasp tightening on the handle of the knife, and I got a shot off just as he raised his arm. But he anticipated it because he jumped behind his son. I watched in rapt fascination as Tad's eyes widened in shock that his father would use him for a shield as the bullet drilled through his chest. Then another. And another. I couldn't say I was surprised the prick sacrificed his son for himself, but I actually felt a little bit sorry for Tad that the final thought he had before he died was that of his father's betrayal.

Grayson tracked Henry as he tried to crawl away. "Freeze!" He didn't stop moving, and a swarm of officers rushed in, assessing the situation. Half turned their attention to Henry, and the other half moved to his son's lifeless body.

Georgia's whimper made me shove my gun away and go to her, frantically freeing her of her bindings. "God, baby, are you okay? I'm so sorry. Are you hurt?" I untied the ropes and lifted her into my arms where she wrapped hers around my neck and burrowed into me. I couldn't believe I let this happen, that there was blood coming from her beautiful body because I wasn't there to save her. I shifted her tighter and vowed silently that nothing like this would ever happen again.

"Hold still." Gray's voice came from behind me, and I heard him tear through the zip ties around her wrists and felt her arms sag in relief.

I wanted to look into her eyes to reassure myself that she was okay, but she needed to burrow into me for strength, so instead of seeing her face, I did what she needed. I held her head and reassured her she was safe as she cried against my chest.

"Can we leave?" She hiccuped, and I was already walking out the door. "Take me home."

"Did she fall asleep easy?" Grayson asked as we stood on my front porch. It had been a few hours since I took Georgia home.

The second we arrived, she wanted to take a shower. I sat on the toilet while she washed her body, and then wrapped her tight in a towel when she finished and bandaged her cut-up wrists from the zip ties. When he cut the seat belt, he got her arm so that had a bandage, too. Aside from that, she had no other injuries, not including the emotional scars this harrowing ordeal would leave her with.

There were loose ends and a bunch of red tape that needed to be dealt with, so I held her hand in the living room when she gave her statement to the detectives, and when she finished, I took her straight to my room, *our room*, and put her to bed.

Everyone had left except Gray, and for the sake of making sure she didn't hear anything else on the chance she was awake, we went outside.

"Yeah, she passed out right away, but who knows how long that'll last."

He nodded tightly. "I get it, man. You need anything else, let me know."

"Thanks, I appreciate that. And I appreciate everything you did. If it wasn't for you telling me he got out, I don't even want to imagine how long it would have taken to figure out who took her."

"Don't mention it."

We shook hands, and I patted him on the back. "Owe you."

He backed away and angled his head at the house. "Go take care of your girl."

"I will."

"And Beau?" I lifted a brow in question. "It wasn't your fault, so stop blaming yourself." He walked away with those parting words, and I didn't bother waiting for him to pull out of the driveway before I went inside, rushing to the bedroom.

She lay on her back, eyes wide open, staring at the blades of the ceiling fan as it spun. "Hey, I thought you were sleeping."

She watched as I got closer, and it wasn't until I lowered myself on the bed that she turned her head. "I was for a second."

"Are you okay, baby?"

"Yes." She swallowed. "I don't want to let them win, not anymore. Tomorrow morning, I might feel differently, but for now, I'm okay."

"You sure? Do you need anything?"

"No. Tad is dead. His father will definitely not be a judge anymore so the Clancys' reign of terror is officially over. I was scared, but in a weird way I felt like I'd been

247

ANNA BROOKS

waiting for it to happen, so I just wanted it to get over with." She released a quavering breath. "I kept thinking about how this was it, but I knew you'd find me and save me, so those thoughts were fleeting. And here I am. Safe. So I'm perfectly fine." She lifted her arm and placed her palm on the side of my face. "Do *you* need anything?"

I pulled my head back at the absurd question. "Why would I?"

"Because I know this is hard on you, and I want to make sure you're okay, too."

My girl, so selfless. I splayed my hand on her collarbone, her strong heart beating against my palm. "I don't need anything, Gigi. I have everything I've ever wanted right here."

CHAPTER 20

Georgia

I SAT AT THE BAR, TWIRLING MY DRINK WITH A STRAW and talking to Jeanie and Bobby. Beau was at the pool table shooting a game with his friend Maverick. Almost every local was here tonight, and all of them came over to wish me well and offer sympathy for what had happened with Tad and his father.

It had been a couple of weeks since that night, and Beau and I had been inseparable. He didn't want to leave my side, and frankly, I needed him near. He took some time off, but he had to go in to work this week, so he arranged for me to have someone with me at all times. I'd enjoyed the forced time to connect with people I otherwise wouldn't have spent eight hours straight with.

When it was Wade's job to sit with me one day, he said something that made me look at my situation, my entire life in a different way. *"There are different lines in life. Some of them are fine, some you don't cross, some you toe the edge of, and some you walk over. But every single one of them requires that you're standing while you do it. You haven't been brought to your knees yet, so there's no way this is what's gonna bring you down."*

He was right. I might have had some setbacks, but nothing stopped me from moving on but me. So I decided to put the past behind me and focus on what was in front of me—Beau.

Because aside from him working, we were together. Like, close enough to touch together, and I loved every second of it. Circumstances beyond our control tore us apart, but we were in command now. We were finally who we were supposed to be this whole time, which was two people meant to be together as one.

Even if I was trying to move forward, I still had a little more anxiety about being kidnapped than I originally thought, but with Beau's assurances and his support, I was ready to start living my life again, our life together, one day at a time. I could tell he was getting a little stir-crazy, too, so we decided to go to The Tap for a drink, and I was glad we did.

"We're gonna leave, sweetie."

I swiveled in my stool and reached over to hug my mom, who was just glowing. "All right. Are you okay to drive, young man?" I pointed at Wade with my eyebrows scrunched together. "You've got precious cargo."

He chuckled and lifted her hand to his mouth and kissed it gently. "Don't I know it."

Seeing them so content was beautiful, and every time I started to feel bitter and angry for all the time Beau and

I lost out on, all I had to do was think about my mom and Wade, and I flipped my perspective to one of gratitude. My focus was on the here and now, and I wanted to make the absolute most of each and every moment Beau and I got to share together.

Wade whistled, and Beau and his brothers, minus Baker, who were hanging out by the pool tables, all gave a manly flick of their fingers to say goodbye.

From across the room, Beau kept an eye on me all night, and I gave him a flirty smile every time I felt him watching, which was often. Excitement started to swirl in my stomach in anticipation of what would happen tonight when we returned home.

As I was turning back around in my stool to finish my conversation with Jeanie, I saw Cheyenne get up from the table she was sitting at with Gage and rush to the bathroom. We hadn't had a chance to get together, and aside from me telling her to rent the house out to someone else and her calling to make sure I was okay, we hadn't had an opportunity to talk.

"Can you watch this, please?" I asked Jeanie as I pushed my drink toward her, then got up and walked to the bathroom.

I opened the door, heard sniffling, and peeked under the doors to find where she was. "Cheyenne, are you okay?"

"Yeah. I'm fine." The toilet flushed, and she came out with red eyes and tearstained cheeks.

"Aw, honey, no, you're not."

She washed her hands, then splashed some water on her face. Grabbing some paper towels to dry her face, she leaned against the wall and crossed her arms. "Tonight was supposed to be fun. Gage and I haven't been on a date in over a year, Georgia. He's only home on weekends, and he just told me he has to leave tomorrow morning instead of tomorrow night like usual." She shook her head. "We get him from like midnight Fridays to about eight on Sundays, and I'm so bummed that he's forfeiting twelve hours of what little time we have together."

"I'm sorry."

She sniffled. "Me too, especially for Lucy."

"I'm here if you need anything, Cheyenne. For you and Lucy. I'm not working yet and honestly don't know if I'll even look for a job since, well... we're not *not* trying but..."

She pulled me in for a hug. "That's awesome, I'm so happy for you."

"Nothing to be happy for yet, and I'm not trying to be selfish when you're struggling, but—"

"I know you're not, I get it. And I appreciate the offer. Who knows, I might take you up on it...and if you're okay with it, I'll add you to Lucy's emergency contacts in case I ever get in a jam."

"Of course I'm okay with it. Listen, Gage is leaving in the morning, so why don't I come over for brunch. I'll bring mimosas, muffins, and face masks. I can get to know Lucy better, and we can have a girl's day."

Her eyes got watery again, and her lip quivered. "I'm so glad you're back."

"Me too."

I hugged her, and once she gathered herself, we returned to the bar. Before I could make my way back to my seat, Beau shouted my name. I gave Cheyenne a little arm squeeze of support and made my way to the pool table. "Yes, dear. You rang?"

"Yeah."

I propped my hands on my hips. "Well, what did you want?"

"You."

I rolled my eyes, and then he hauled me into his arms and gave me a loud, smacking kiss. "Get a room." Bear shoved Beau in the shoulder, and I felt his lips turn up to a smile against my skin.

He tossed back the rest of his beer and began pulling me toward the exit. "That's actually a good idea."

"What are you doing?"

"Getting a room."

"What?" I laughed as I tried to wave with my free hand, and when we got outside, he pushed me against the brick and kissed me deep, his fingers massaging my butt as he rubbed me against his hard crotch. "Where are we going?" I asked breathlessly.

"I have something to show you."

"What? Where?"

He winked. "It's a surprise. Come on."

I followed as he led me to his truck, and as he was

backing away, he turned the radio off. His thumb was tapping on the steering wheel, and he was bouncing his left leg. It was making me nervous. "Is everything okay? You seem... I don't know, antsy or something."

"Everything's great, babe." He took my hand in his and rubbed his thumb over my pulse point as he steered us toward the outskirts of town.

Beau turned down a dirt road, then made a left and stopped, the headlights pointing toward an empty field. "Come on." He shut the engine off but left the lights on, then came over to my side and helped me down.

"What is this, Beau?"

"Yours, if you want it."

I pulled my head back and looked up at him in utter confusion. "What are you talking about?"

He linked our fingers and started walking down the dirt path. "When I built my house, I did it with the idea, the hope, that you'd eventually live in it, and our kids would grow up in it. And it's got enough room for all that, but I know you feel like it's not ours. And I want our house to feel like *our home*."

"I love what you built, Beau."

"I do, too, but I think we'd both love building something from the ground up together. Every memory we'd have of a new place would be with us together. I want your input on the layout and your touch on the design. I want you to make it exactly how you want it. I... I want you to love it so much that you'll never leave it."

My heart crumbled at his vulnerability, and I touched

our toes as I moved in front of him and rested my hands on his chest. "I'm never leaving you, Beau." His jaw clenched, and he looked over my head. "Hey, look at me." I got his eyes back, and I cradled his face. "I promise I'm not going anywhere ever unless it's with you. And I don't need to build a new house. We don't need to waste time worrying about contractors and design when we should be focusing on making a family and—"

He bent his neck and cut my words off with a kiss, swinging me up into his arms and lifting me against him. The door to his truck creaked, and he laid me on the bench seat. "I wanted you so bad back then. Right here." He splayed his hands flat on my stomach and slid them under my shirt. His thumb brushed over my nipple, and it pebbled under his touch. "Wanted to kiss you." He slid my shirt up and kissed my stomach. "Touch you." He grabbed my bra along with the hem of my shirt and pushed them both up to my neck. Then his fingers trailed softly under my breasts, and I arched into him. "Taste you." His mouth closed over one nipple while he rolled the other with his fingers.

"God, Beau." I squirmed, the tight confines of the truck heightening my senses.

"And now I can." He switched breasts and rolled his tongue before releasing the hypersensitive skin with a pop. "Now I can do it all whenever I want, can't I?"

I sank my fingers into his hair. "Yes, Beau."

He whipped off my top and bra and pulled his shirt over his head before settling his weight on me. His warm, muscled chest pressing against mine while he kissed me made the backs of my knees tingle. He tilted his head, caressing my mouth slow and deep, claiming in a way he never had before.

I ran my nails down his back, pressure getting harder as I got lower. My fingers dipped below the waistband of his boxer briefs, and he sat up, his hand going to his belt buckle. "Wiggle your shorts down as far as you can, babe. I need to get in there."

"Hurry," I panted as I tore my zipper down and watched him do the same. I got them as far as my knees, and his jeans were to his ankles before he slid his hands behind my back and maneuvered us so he was sitting and I straddled him.

"Take 'em off." He shoved at my shorts, and I had to kick a shoe off to be able to straddle him, and before I could get the other one off, he held my waist with one hand while the other went to his hard cock, and he thrust up and pushed me down. "Fuck."

"Oh my God." I fell back, my hands finding purchase on his knees.

He lifted his face to mine, and a moan slid up my throat at the heated look in his eyes. He wrapped his hands around my neck, his thumbs against my jaw. "Ride me, Gigi. Fuck your man."

It didn't matter that we'd never done this position before because moving on him was second nature. I rolled my hips, circled, bounced...; I went slow, then fast, always deep. My eyes got heavy, and my thighs burned, but

I couldn't stop. "You feel so good," I panted on a downward glide. "Shit, Beau, it's so good."

"I know it is, baby. Keep fuckin' me as long as you can. Work my cock with that sweet pussy." I grunted as I moved faster, the waves of pleasure pulling me under. "Fuck, I can feel that."

"I... God, I'm gonna come."

He tilted my head down, and my eyes fluttered opened to see his face. His eyes dark, lips snarled, and a bead of sweat rolling down his temple. "Look at me when you milk my cock dry, Gigi. Watch what you do to me."

"Yes, yes, God, yes!" Tremors shook my body, and I tried to keep my eyes open, but the pleasure was too much. My pussy spasmed so hard, and my thighs clamped so tight that I knew I'd be sore tomorrow, but I didn't care.

"Fuck, Georgia," Beau growled, and dug his fingers into my hips while he pistoned his up and fucked me harder than I ever could.

He hit a spot that made me scream, and I came again while I was still coming the first time. "It's too much," I gasped as my body went to another dimension, and I saw stars.

"Never enough. Not ever enough with you." He pulled me down and groaned, long and low, and I felt him spill inside me. "Fuck, fuck, fuck."

I collapsed on top of him and listened as his breath evened out. His truck smelled of sex and sweat, and I loved it. I loved *him*. "That was... that was amazing," I whispered.

He chuckled. "Never felt anything like it in my life. Not sure amazing is the word I'd use."

My heart, already swelled, got fuller knowing I gave him something nobody else had. "What word would you use?"

"Indescribable."

I giggled and felt him shift beneath me a little bit, then heard something ruffling before he pried my hand out of his hair. I sat up to look down at him, but instead, my eyes caught on the sparkling ring he was sliding on my finger. "You don't even need to ask because you know my answer will be yes."

He ran his thumb gently over the ring to center it, and his lips tilted up in a soft smile as he brought his gaze to me. "I wasn't going to."

I giggled, and for the first time since those two months with him, I was at peace. I was free and hopeful. I was happy.

And now I was engaged, and I was pretty sure that was also the night I got pregnant.

EPILOGUE

Georgia

Six months later.

"**D**O YOU TAKE THIS WOMAN TO BE YOUR lawfully wedded wife…" As the officiant read the vows, his voice distorted into fuzzy background noise as I gazed into Beau's eyes.

He stared back and mouthed, "I love you."

"Love you, too," I whispered back.

"Do you have the ring?" The officiant had to raise his voice at Beau. "Sir, do you have the ring?"

"Yeah, sorry." He dug into his pocket, pulled his hand out empty, and then frantically patted his suit coat. "Uhh…"

"Son," Wade snapped, and Beau lifted his head, smirking at his father. "Just kidding."

The guests laughed as Beau handed the ring to his dad, and I looked up at my mother, whose face was lit up with a happiness I'd never seen before. The same happiness I felt every morning when I woke up with Beau.

Wade slid the diamond on her finger, and I couldn't hold back the tears that fell.

Beau watched and cleared his throat, then dropped his head and shuffled his feet from side to side.

"By the powers vested in me, I now pronounce you husband and wife. Wade, you may kiss your bride."

I don't care how old you are. Watching your mom make out with someone was gross, and I scrunched my nose, and all the Bradford brothers made a dramatic gagging sound and covered their eyes. The newlyweds walked down the aisle toward where the outdoor reception was being held on the beautiful Ryder Ranch property, and the guests got up to follow.

I loved that they were happy and finally found their way to each other even after decades apart. The way some things in life worked out was amazing. Simply amazing. I felt a flutter in my stomach and put my hand over my belly. Beau's awareness heightened and he was by my side in a split second. "You okay?"

"Yes, honey." I moved my hand as he put his on my belly. "I honestly think I'm just hungry. Everything is fine."

"God, I love you."

"I know you do."

We both looked over when there was a whoop from the reception. Bear spun my mom in a circle, and her laughter echoed all the way over here.

Beau lifted my hand, kissing the ring on my finger. "Are you sure you don't want any of this?" He motioned around at the food and music and plethora of people.

A month after everything had happened, Beau and I went to the courthouse and got hitched. Just the two of us with my mom and his dad as witnesses. I didn't want a big wedding or a party or anything. I just wanted to be married to him. And because he's so amazing, he gave me that. On the other hand, our parents wanted something to celebrate their second chance, and that's definitely what they got.

"I'm sure." I angled my head. "All I ever wanted was you, Beau."

"Good thing you've got me, then." He dipped his head and kissed me. "Let's get you fed." Beau kissed my temple, and I nodded eagerly. I was starving. We started heading toward the delicious smell of barbecue, but Wade walked up to us and grabbed Beau, hugging him tight.

The past several months had been challenging as everyone adjusted to the events and how they happened. Two couples reuniting because of circumstances beyond their control wasn't something that just went smoothly. There was a lot of guilt from all parties and regret that wouldn't ever go away, but as time went on, hopefully those feelings would lessen.

"Wish your brother was here."

There'd also been anger. Baker packed a bag and left the day after I was kidnapped and hadn't returned since. Not even for his father's wedding.

"He'll be back, Pop." Beau pulled away from his dad and clasped his arm. "You know Baker. He's the wild child.

261

He was the one affected the most by Mom's death, and you moving on feels like a betrayal to him."

"But I—"

Beau cut him off. "It's not. You're allowed to move on and be happy. He'll get over it and come back after he gets some of the anger out of his system."

Brody arrived two days ago, and even though Baker had been staying with him out in California, they didn't come together.

"I hope so."

"Hey, Wade." My mom came up and rested her hand on his arm.

"Yes, my Belle?"

Her face still lit up when he called her that. "We're supposed to go cut the cake now."

"Then let's go."

Mom's smile turned embarrassed, and I laughed when I saw Wade cop a feel through her ivory dress.

"Did he just grab her butt?" I asked my husband.

"I'm going to pretend I didn't see that."

"Yeah." I rested my head on Beau's chest. "It's going to take a lot of time to get used to them being together, but I'm thrilled they finally found their happy." I gave him a squeeze. "Like us."

He grasped my chin and tilted my head back. "I didn't have to get used to you because even when you weren't here, you never left me, not even for a second."

"You either."

"I dreamed about a life with you for so long I was

starting to think it'd never happen. But now that I have it, I couldn't imagine one without you." He stared into my eyes, his voice gruff with emotion. "If you left again, Gigi, I wouldn't survive. I need you to complete the part of me that was always missing because you make me whole. And I promise you, honey, I'll do everything in my power to make you feel the same for the rest of your life."

And as his lips claimed mine, I knew he always would.

ABOUT THE AUTHOR

The first time Anna tried to read a romance novel, her hair caught on fire when she leaned over a candle to sneak a peek at her mom's Harlequin. She thinks being hit on the head with a shirtless Fabio until the smoke cleared is what sparked the flame for her love of romance.

Anna was born in Wisconsin, but lives in Texas with her husband and two boys. She writes sexy romance that always has a happy ending and loves bringing characters back for cameos. Less than six degrees of separation connects any of her novels.

When she's not writing or reading, she's watching reruns of her favorite romcoms, talking to her dogs and cat like they're human, eating carbs, or practicing hand lettering.

She loves to hear from readers and can be found on social media as @annabrooksauth everywhere, or you can contact her from her website annabrooksauthor.com/contact

OTHER BOOKS BY ANNA

It's Kind Of Personal Series
Make Me Forget
Show Me How
Prove Me Right
Tell Me When
Remember Me Now
Give Me This

Pleasant Valley Series
Fixing Fate
Love, Me
Steady

Bulletproof Butterfly Series
Easy Sacrifice
Bulletproof Butterfly
Heartbreaker
Guarding Georgia